Georgia Dept. of Agriculture

Georgia

from the immigrant settler's stand-point. Giving the results of the

experience of actual settlers from other states and countries, prefaced

with an account of the natural resources of Georgia, and the inducements

to immigrants and capitalist

Georgia Dept. of Agriculture

Georgia

from the immigrant settler's stand-point. Giving the results of the experience of actual settlers from other states and countries, prefaced with an account of the natural resources of Georgia, and the inducements to immigrants and capitalist

ISBN/EAN: 9783337239039

Printed in Europe, USA, Canada, Australia, Japan

Cover: Foto ©Andreas Hilbeck / pixelio.de

More available books at **www.hansebooks.com**

From the Immigrant Settler's Stand-Point.

GIVING THE RESULTS OF THE EXPERIENCE OF ACT-
UAL SETTLERS FROM OTHER STATES AND COUN-
TRIES, PREFACED WITH AN ACCOUNT OF THE
NATURAL RESOURCES OF GEORGIA,
AND THE INDUCEMENTS TO IMMI-
GRANTS AND CAPITALISTS

PREPARED UNDER THE DIRECTION OF

THOMAS P. JANES, A.M., M.D.,

COMMISSIONER OF AGRICULTURE OF GEORGIA.

ATLANTA, GA.:
1879.

PREFACE.

The South has been misunderstood and often misrepresented—sometimes by immigration agents of other States, often by designing politicians and partisan newspapers, and occasionally by those, who, having travelled through the country, are therefore presumed to know whereof they affirm.

These misconceptions and misrepresentations have not been confined to the sentiments of our people, but have had reference also to our habits, our customs, our administration and observance of law, the general condition of society, and also to our natural advantages of climate, soil, productions, etc., a correct knowledge of which is so essential to the intending emigrant, if we would attract him to our borders.

These errors have often been corrected, and unjust charges denied, but, as might reasonably have been feared—from the presumed partiality of our writers and speakers—without fully vindicating our section and people in the minds of a large number of those who are honestly seeking the truth.

With a view to clearly setting forth the natural advantages of the State of Georgia as a home for the immigrant, and the inducements offered for safe and profitable investments of capital, the *Commissoner of Agriculture* prepared and published, in 1878, "A MANUAL OF GEORGIA, *for the use of Immigrants and Capitalists.*" A large number of copies of this MANUAL were distributed throughout the North and West, and some have been sent to Europe, with the effect of increasing the interest already aroused in the minds of those who contemplate emigrating, and are on the lookout for the State which affords the greatest natural inducements and other attractions.

The *Manual of Georgia*, though giving an accurate and exhaustive description of the State by counties, would have been still more valuable for the purpose intended, had it contained some accounts of the experience of those who have settled in the State within the last fifteen years. It is intended to supply this testimony by publishing "*Georgia, from the Immigrant Settler's standpoint.*"

In the preparation of the pamphlet a circular letter was sent to one or more of the regular correspondents of the Department of Agriculture in each of the counties of the State, requesting them to furnish the names of several of the most intelligent and reliable citizens of their respective counties who were born and reared in the North or a foreign country, and have, *since* 1865, immigrated to, and become permanent citizens of the State. In response to this circular, the names and postoffice address of one or more such citizens was supplied from a sufficient number of counties to fairly represent every section of the State. To those, a circular, a copy of which appears in Part II., was sent, and the replies are appended immediately following the description of the several sections of the State.

As this publication will fall into the hands of many who have not read the MANUAL OF GEORGIA, it has been thought best to embody in PART I. much of the general information contained in the latter work, and which is not supplied by the published letters from actual settlers.

Those who may wish to verify the authenticity of the published letters, or obtain further information from the same source, are invited to write to the authors, many of whom have voluntarily signified their willingness to respond to any enquiries which they may receive.

It is proper to remark, in conclusion, that this publication has been prepared for the sole purpose of advancing the material interests of Georgia, by encouraging the immigration of honest, sober, industrious citizens from every section of the Union and from the most desirable nationalities of Europe.

THOMAS P. JANES,
Commissioner of Agriculture.

Atlanta, Ga., July 22, 1879.

NOTE. For more detailed information and statistics of the several counties of the State, the reader is referred to "A MANUAL OF GEORGIA, *for the Use of Immigrants and Capitalists*," a copy of which will be sent by mail to any applicant enclosing a 3 cent stamp for return postage.

PART I.

GEOGRAPHICAL SITUATION OF GEORGIA.

The State of Georgia lies in the southeastern portion of the United States, and, with Florida, constitutes the extreme portion of the American Union in that direction. In the original settlement, its chartered limits extended from the Atlantic ocean to the Mississippi river, with the 31st parallel of north latitude as its northern boundary, and the 31st parallel and Florida as its boundary on the South. Early in the present century, a very large portion of this territory westward—nearly two-thirds—was ceded to the United States, and out of it, in great part, have since been formed the two new States of Alabama and Mississippi.

From the above, it will be seen that the entire State lies within the southern portion of the temperate zone, and, as a consequence, is exempt alike from the rigors and other discomforts and disadvantages of a cold climate, and the debility and diseases incident to tropical regions. It may be said with perfect truth, that there is no part of the known world where a greater degree of physical comfort can be secured the year round, or where a greater amount of labor can be performed in the usual vocations, within the same period of time, than in Georgia. But these points will be more fully treated under their appropriate heads.

The geographical situation of Georgia is worthy of note in another, the commercial view of the question. The 32d parallel of north latitude passes nearly through the centre of the State; the great southern trans-continental line of railway, to connect the Atlantic and Pacific oceans by a communication uninterruped by snows in winter, and open the year round, has been located on and near that parallel. Savannah, Georgia's principal seaport, is but 15′ north of that line, and is destined to become the eastern terminus of this great highway of trade. It is 943 miles nearer to San Diego, on the California coast, than New York—the eastern terminus of the northern lines—is to San Francisco; the distance between the two latter cities being 3,456 miles, while the distance between the two former is only 2,512 miles. This road will be completed in a very few years, and its beneficial effects upon the trade and general prosperity of Georgia are too obvious to require comment. The facts stated show that this southern line is destined to become the favorite highway of the Pacific trade, including that of China and Japan, with the ports of Georgia as its chief *entrepots* in the East.

Georgia, from her geographical relations, is also the natural highway to the teeming products of the great agricultural heart of the country—the Mississippi Valley. A straight line from St. Louis, or the mouth of the Ohio, shows that the Atlantic coast of Georgia is much nearer and more accessible to the commerce of the West than that of any other State in the Union. Several lines of railway between these two sections are already in successful operation; while a projected canal from the Tennessee river to the head of navigation on the Altamaha tributaries in Georgia will afford ample water transportation to the commerce of the West seeking European markets, and, in point of time, speedier than that hitherto employed—the circuitous route *via* the Mississippi river and the Gulf of Mexico. This canal route has been surveyed by direction of Congress, its practicability and cheapness fully determined, and its construction made a simple question of time.

FACE OF THE COUNTRY.

The nominal divisions of the State are three-fold, to wit: Lower, Middle and Upper Georgia. These correspond, in the order stated, with the three great natural divisions, viz: the low country, the hill country and the mountain region.

Lower Georgia lies below the line crossing the heads of navigation of the rivers, a portion of which flow into the Atlantic ocean, and a portion into the Gulf of Mexico. It is the largest of the three divisions, comprising about 35,000 square miles. It lies for the most part, below the level of 300 feet above the sea, the average elevation being about 250 feet.

Middle Georgia lies between the heads of navigation and the elevation of 1,000 or 1,100 feet, the average being 750 feet. It has an area of 15,000 square miles.

Upper Georgia constitutes the northern portion of the State, and embraces all the mountains of any note, and much hill country. It has an area of about 10,000 square miles. The eastern half has an average elevation of about 1,500 feet, whilst there are mountain chains that rise to the height of 3,000 feet, and peaks to 4,800 feet. The western half is much lower, the general elevation being only 750 feet, with mountains up to 2,000 feet.

The average elevation of the surface of the State is 650 feet above the sea.

These three divisions of the State differ in soil and climate, and, to some extent, in productions, as we shall have occasion to note more particularly hereafter, when we come to treat of those several topics.

CLIMATE.

In nothing regarding us, is a greater mistake made abroad and indeed, in some parts of our own country, than in the climate, or atmospheric conditions, of Georgia. The State being in the southern portion of the Union, lying between parallels of latitudes 30°, 39′, 27″ (average) and 35°, the stranger naturally concludes that our climate is mild and delightful in Winter; and in this he is correct. We have but little snow—in more than half the States none at all for years together—we import or manufacture all our ice, and field work may be kept up at all periods of the year. The difficulty with strangers is in determining the character of our climate during the summer months. The winters being pleasant and genial, they conclude, without further investigation, that the summers must necessarily be hot and sultry. This is a serious mistake, as all will testify who have any practical knowledge of the subject. No finer summer climate is to be found on the continent, east of the Mississippi river, than that of many parts of Georgia, and, as a whole, it will compare favorably in this respect with that of the States of the north and northwest. Carefully conducted observations, year after year, shows that the mean annual temperature of the city of Atlanta, our State Capital, is the same with that of Washington City, Louisville, Kentucky, and St. Louis, in the State of Missouri, which are from 800 to 880 miles further north. The mean annual temperature south of a line drawn across the State from Augusta to Columbus, is between 64° and 68°; between the same line and another parallel to it, and running twenty miles south of Atlanta, we have a mean annual temperature between 60° and 64°; in another strip of territory including Atlanta, we have a mean temperature the year round of between 56° and 60°. In that we have described as Upper Georgia, it is between 52° and 56°, while in the mountains it is below 52°. The mean of Gainesville, in Hall county, and of Clarksville and Mount Airy, in Habersham county, corresponds with that of Central Ohio, Indiana, Illinois, Upper Missouri and Lower Nebraska. We refer to the map of the State for a better understanding of the several localities above referred to, as well as the significance of the figures given in this connection. We have the winter climate of Rome, and the summer climate of Jerusalem.

SOILS AND PRODUCTIONS.

The soils of Georgia are among the very best of the older States ; in virgin fertility she surpassed them all, as is evidenced by her rapid settlement from other States upon the extinguishment of the

Indian title to the lands.   Injudicious cultivation, in the haste to get rich, has done much, in past years, to impair and waste their strength; but wiser views are now obtaining, and with systems of culture greatly improved, production is steadily increasing without material addition to the population.

The soils of Georgia are as various as the elements of rocks, and the vegetable and animal remains that compose them.

In Upper Georgia, or the northern-most division of the State, the soil is a mixture of clay and sand.   In the western half of this section there is a large admixture of lime, and the clay is generally red, with here and there a yellowish brown or drab.   In the eastern half, the clay is altogether reddish, and the soil not calcareous.   The valley and coves of both are very rich and productive, while the hill-sides yield generously to judicious cultivation. There are many fine farms on the very summit of the Blue Ridge and Lookout range of mountains.

The chief agricultural productions of Upper Georgia are Indian corn or maize, wheat, barley, rye, oats, potatoes, sorghum and all the grasses, including clover.   Its wheat, with that of Middle Georgia, is considered the heaviest and best grown in the Union, and always commands a premium in the Northern markets.   All the grains mentioned grow to great perfection, and the yield of hay, where proper attention is given that crop, is very large.   The soil and climate are also admirably adapted to tobacco, though it has not, up to this time, received that attention as a crop that it deserves.   Many good judges consider Upper Georgia, in this respect, superior to either Virginia or North Carolina, as the soil is not only suitable, but the season for planting is much earlier, and of growth longer, enabling the farmer to gather a second crop from the same plants.   Until a very recent date, this section of the State was regarded as unsuited to the successful cultivation of cotton, but the introduction of commercial fertilizers, the effect of which is to hasten growth and maturity and increase production, has brought about quite a revolution as regards the great staple. It is now being successfully grown, in considerable quantities, as far north as the Tennessee line.   As evidence of the rapid increase in the production of cotton in this section, we may mention the fact that the city of Atlanta, whose trade in that commodity ten years ago was so inconsiderable as scarcely to have a place in the local market reports, had received, up to the first of April of the present year (1878), or in seven out of the twelve cotton months, 98,000 bales, grown almost exclusively in Upper Georgia.   Hemp, flax and jute may also be grown with profit.   During a good part of the year the mountains afford the finest range for cattle, sheep and goats, whilst hogs keep fat in the fall and early winter months on the masts of nuts and acorns. All the varieties of vegetables flourish in this part of the State. The fruits that thrive best are the apple, the pear, the cherry, the plum and the grape; also the raspberry and strawberry. The last mentioned may be said to grow equally well in every part of the State. The spring and well water of this section is unsurpassed in any part of the world.

The surface of Middle Georgia is rolling, and the soil generally red, with here and there a liberal admixture of gray, and very strong and productive. All things considered, this is regarded as the most desirable portion of the State, if not of the South. It is the great cotton section, or the section where the soil will yield a greater amount of fruit than a like area of equal fertility in any other part of the State. Indian corn, wheat, barley, rye—indeed, all the cereal crops—are cultivated, and yield in their greatest abundance. Even the oldest lands of this section recuperate rapidly under good treatment, and are soon restored to their original fertility. Improved systems of culture are obtaining very generally throughout this part of the State, which is the most populous of the three great divisions, and, as a consequence, production is progressive. Of fruits, the apple, pear, peach, fig, grape, melons, and indeed every variety, other than tropical, are grown with the greatest success. The finest peaches in the world grow in this section and in the northern portion of Lower Georgia, and large quantities are shipped annually to the northern cities. Melons, also, are grown to great perfection, and constitute quite an important item of the commerce of this section. The forests and abandoned fields abound in nuts and berries in large variety, furnished by nature without care or cultivation. Dried fruits are becoming an important item in the exports from this section.

It may be said with truth that no country in the world offers greater natural advantages than this middle section of Georgia. Embracing a territory about two hundred miles in length from east to west, and one hundred broad from north to south, intersected by numerous rivers and smaller water courses, the amount of water power available for manufacturing purposes is incalculable. It constitutes the heart of the cotton region, and the material is consequently at hand to be worked into the various fabrics. Ten railroads cross it in various directions, so that transportation is all that could be desired. Its drinking water is excellent, and its health uninterrupted throughout the year.

Southern, or Lower Georgia, consists chiefly of sandy, pine land, with occasional belts of oak and hickory, and where these occur the soil has a considerable mixture of reddish or light-brown clay, and is very productive. The lands generally are light and easy of cultivation, and while some portions, especially those on the water courses of the southwest and the red lands above referred to, are very rich, nearly the whole is tillable, and, with occasional light manuring, continue to produce good crops from year to year. It is, as a general rule, sparsely settled, and the lands are the cheapest in the State. The leading field products are cotton, sugar cane, corn, rice, oats, potatoes and field peas. The country being open, and the pasturage good throughout the year, large numbers of beef cattle and sheep are raised annually for market, at a cost purely nominal, as they require neither to be fed nor sheltered. Wool forms quite an item in the list of its exports; near 75,000 pounds were cleared at the custom-house in Brunswick alone during the past year.

Cotton is produced generally throughout the section—the sea-island, or long staple variety, in the counties bordering on Florida and along the coast. This class of cotton is used in the manufacture of the finer fabrics, and in combination with silk, but is less cultivated than in former years, the demand for it having been lessened by the improvement in the staple and quality of the common cotton, and in the machinery for its manufacture.

The cotton crop of Georgia averages a little over 500,000 bales, or about 225,000,000 pounds, worth, at ten cents per pound, $22,500,000.

The rice lands lie chiefly on the tide water, and are among the most valuable and productive on the southern coast. Considerable rice is also grown, chiefly for home consumption, on inland swamps and low lands in Middle as well as in Lower Georgia, though the rice that enters into commerce comes chiefly from the country along the coast.

Sugar cane is also an important crop of Southern Georgia, and could be made among the most profitable. It grows luxuriantly, and yields profitable returns in sugar and syrup. Yet, but little sugar is made for market, the planters usually confining themselves to a sufficiency for home demand, and relying chiefly upon the syrup as a marketable crop. To show the capacity of the soil under high culture, we mention one instance among the many of equal production that are well vouched for. In 1874, Mr. John J. Parker, of Thomas county, produced, on one acre, 694⅓ gallons of cane syrup, worth seventy-five cents per gallon, or $520.87. The total cost of production was $77.50, leaving a net profit of $443.37.

This section of the State also produces an excellent quality of light tobacco, such as is manufactured into cigars, though the plant will eventually run into the heavy leaf unless the seed are renewed annually from the West Indies.

Notwithstanding the variety of soils and climates, vegetables of every description do well in all parts of the State; but it is chiefly in the section along the coast that they are raised for distant markets. Most of the varieties maturing here in early spring, before the seeds are planted in the Northern States of the Union, they command a good price in consequence, and the producers realize large profits from their business. In the spring of 1877 there were shipped to the Northern markets, from the port of Savannah alone, 23,284 packages of fruit, 20,405 packages of vegetable and 26,345 melons.

Of the fruits of this section, melons, strawberries, grapes and some oranges, are those chiefly cultivated for market. The fig and grape grow to great perfection, and the orange, lemon, lime, banana, pomegranate, of the tropical fruits, succeed well where attention has been given to their cultivation. Some varieties of the pear also thrive well in this section of the State. The Scuppernong grape grows in its greatest perfection; the crops are very heavy, and the fruit sweeter than that grown in more northern latitudes.

Lower Georgia is said to resemble, in soil and climate, those portions of Prussia that lie in the vicinity of the capital. The soil is, however, in its natural state, far more productive, and consequently requires less labor and expense to be kept in good planting condition. Although generally sandy, it has a good clay foundation, or subsoil, from six to twelve inches below the surface, which enables it to retain fertilizers and hold them as plant food.

CAPACITY OF GEORGIA SOIL UNDER HIGH CULTURE.

The various agricultural products common to Georgia having been given with some minuteness in the chapter on Soils and Productions, we proceed to give the results of a number of experiments in the cultivation of those products, in each of those divisions, conducted with proper preparation and fertilization—such as are given in the more densely settled portions of the world. As but little is accomplished by inadequate means in any department of human industry, the actual producing capacity of a country can only be tested by the results of *judicious* culture. The crops, to which we shall refer, were reported to the various State and county fairs within the past few years, and both the culture and its results were verified by the affidavits of disinterested parties.

In 1873, Mr. R. H. Hardaway produced, on upland, in Thomas county, (Lower Georgia) 119 bushels of Indian corn on one acre, which yielded a net profit of $77.17.

In the same county, the same year, Mr. E. T. Davis produced

96½ bushels of rust-proof oats per acre. After the oats were harvested he planted the same land in cotton, and in the fall gathered 800 pounds of seed cotton.

Mr. John J. Parker, of the same county, produced, in 1874, on one acre, 694½ gallons of cane syrup, at a cost of $77.50. The syrup, at 75 cents per gallon, the market price, brought $520.87—net profit from one acre, $443.37.

In 1874, Mr. Wiley W. Groover, of Brooks county, (Lower Georgia) produced, with two horses, on a farm of 126½ acres, without the aid of commercial fertilizers, cotton, corn, oats, peas, sugar cane and potatoes to the value of $3,258.25. The total cost of production was $1,045.00, leaving net proceeds of crop, $2,213.25. The stock raised on the farm was not counted.

Joseph Hodges, of the same county, produced, on one acre, 2,700 pounds of seed cotton; Wm. Borden, 600 gallons of syrup; J. Bower, 500 bushels of sweet potatoes; J. O. Morton, 75 bushels oats. Mr. T. W. Jones made 12 barrels, or 480 gallons of syrup on one acre, and saved enough cane for seed.

In Bulloch county, (Lower Georgia) 3,500 pounds seed cotton were produced by Samuel Groover, and in the same county 21 barrels sugar at one time, and 700 gallons syrup at another, per acre.

In Clay county, Mr. —— Hodge produced from one acre, a few years ago, 4,500 pounds of seed cotton.

Mr J. R. Respass, of Schley county, gathered the present year (1878) a little upwards of 500 bushels of oats from five acres.

Mr. J. R. Respass, of Schley county, (Lower Georgia) in 1877, by the use of fertilizers, grew on five acres of naturally poor land, 15,000 pounds of seed cotton, which netted him when sold $66.02 per acre.

Mr. H. T. Peeples, of Berrien county, reports to this Department a crop of 800 bushels of sweet potatoes grown on one acre of pine land.

In 1876, Mr. G. J. Drake, of Spalding county, (Middle Georgia) produced 74 bushels of corn on one acre of land.

Mr John Bonner, of Carroll county, made three bales of cotton (500 pounds each) on one acre. Mr. R. H. Springer, of the same county, produced nine bales from five acres, without manures, and ninety-four bales from 100 acres, by the use of fertilizers.

In 1873, Mr. S. W. Leak, of the same county, produced on one acre 40½ bushels of wheat, worth $80.50; cost $14.50—net profit $66.00.

In Wilkes county 123 bushels corn were produced on one acre of bottom land; also 42 bushels Irish potatoes on one-tenth acre, the second crop same year on same land; the first crop very fine, but not so good.

Mr. J. F. Madden, of the same county, produced, in 1876, on one acre, 137 bushels of oats.

Mr. T. C. Warthen, of Washington county, (on the line of Middle and Lower Georgia) produced in 1873, on 1.1125 acres, 6,917 pounds of seed cotton, equivalent to five bales of 461 pounds each, worth, at 17½ cents per pound—the average price of that year—$403.37. The cost of culture was $148.58; net profit, $254.79, for a very small fraction over one acre.

Dr. Wm. Jones, of Burke county, produced 480 gallons syrup on one acre. Wesley Jones, of the same county, produced three bales of cotton, 500 pounds each, per acre. Jas. J. Davis, in same county, made, in 1877, with two mules, thirty-four bales of cotton, 500 pounds each, 600 bushels corn, and 300 bushels oats. Wm. C. Palmer, of same county, made, in 1877, with one mule, twenty-five bales of cotton, 500 pounds each, and a fair crop of corn. Henry Miller, of same county, produced, in 1877, sixty-five bushels corn per acre, first year, on reclaimed swamp, without manures.

Mr. R. M. Brooks, of Pike county, (Middle Georgia) produced, in 1873, on five acres of bottom land, 500 bushels of rice. The total cost was $75—net profit, $300.

Mr. R. B. Baxter, of Hancock county, (Middle Georgia) in 1872, harvested at the first cutting, first year's crop, 4,862 pounds of dry clover hay per acre.

Mr. A. J. Preston, of Crawford county, gathered, from one acre of Flint river bottom, 4,000 pounds seed cotton, and from another, on same place, 115 bushels corn.

Dr. T. P. Janes, of Greene county, (Middle Georgia) produced, in 1871, five tons of clover hay per acre, in one season, at two cuttings.

Mr. Patrick Long, of Bibb county, (on the line of Middle and Lower Georgia) harvested from one acre of land, from which he had gathered a crop of cabbages in June of the same year, 8,646 pounds of native crab-grass hay.

Mr. S. W. Leak, in Spalding county, (Middle Georgia) gathered, in the fall of 1873, from one acre, from which he had harvested forty bushels of wheat in June, 10,720 pounds of pea-vine hay. Net profit from wheat, $66; from pea-vine hay, $233.08, making in one year from a single acre, a net profit of $299.08.

Mr. William Smith, of Coweta county, (Middle Georgia) produced 2,200 pounds seed cotton per acre on ten acres.

Mr. Edward Camp, of the same county, produced 1,000 bushels oats from ten acres.

Mr. J. T. Manley of Spalding county, (Middle Georgia) produced 115 bushels of oats from one acre.

Mr. S. W. Bloodworth, of the same county, gathered, in 1870, 137 bushels of corn from one acre.

Mr. L. B. Willis, in Greene county, (Middle Georgia) in June, 1873, from one acre and a third, harvested twenty bushels of wheat, and the following October, 27,130 pounds of corn forage. From the forage alone he received a profit of $159.22 per acre.

Dr. W. Moody of the same county, harvested, at one cutting, from one acre of river bottom, in 1874, 13,953 pounds of Bermuda grass hay; cost, $12.87, value of hay, $209.29, net profit, $196.42.

Mr. J. R. Winters, of Cobb county, (Upper Georgia) produced, in 1873, from 1.15 acres, 6,575 pounds of dry clover hay at the first cutting of the second year's crop.

Mr. T. H. Moore, of same county, produced on one acre 105 bushels of corn, while Mr. Jeremiah Daniel produced 125 bushels,

Mr. R. Peters, Jr., of Gordon county, (Upper Georgia) harvested, in 1874, from three acres of lucerne, four years old, fourteen tons and 200 pounds of hay, or 9,400 pounds per acre.

Capt. C. W. Howard produced, on Lookout Mountain, in Walker county, (Upper Georgia) in 1874, on one acre of unmanured land,. which cost him twenty-five cents per acre, with one hoeing and plowing, 108½ bushels of Irish potatoes, which he sold in Atlanta at a net profit of $97.25. On land manured and better prepared and worked, double that quantity could be produced.

Mr. Thomas Smith, of Cherokee county, produced 104 bushels of corn from one acre.

Mr. John Dyer, of Bibb county, produced, in 1873, from one acre, at a cost of $8.00, 398.7 bushels of sweet potatoes, which he sold at a net profit of $290.92.

Mr. Haddon P. Redding, of Fulton county, in 1877, produced from one acre 400 bushels of St. Domingo yam potatoes, which he readily sold in Atlanta at an average price of $1.00 a bushel.

These instances of production are exceptional, and far beyond the usual results of farming in our State; but they serve to show the capacity of our soil when properly fertilized, and cultivated with intelligence under the guidance of science. It will not be denied, however, that what the parties named have accomplished on a limited scale, may be done by others on still larger areas, and with corresponding results.

METALS AND MINERALS OF GEORGIA.

It is conceded by all who have any adequate information on the subject, that the mineral resources of Georgia, in extent and value, are unsurpassed, if equalled, by those of any other American State.

The variety and richness of her ores, and other natural products of a kindred nature, are facts which, in their full force, have lain buried beneath the earth's surface until recent scientific explorations under the direction of the state government, brought them to the light. It being impossible, without too great elaboration, to go through the long catalogue of specimens that lie exposed to view on the shelves of our Geological Museum, we shall confine our observations to a few leading products, which will fully establish the position that, to the miner, no country on the globe presents advantages superior to those of Georgia.

Gold.—It is impossible to estimate the true value of this interest, and all calculations must be based upon the actual production of the mines in the past, and indications of the presence of that precious metal as they appear to the scientific eye. These are the only reliable data, and we shall limit our remarks to what they will fully justify.

Dr. George Little, State Geologist, after a thorough exploration of the auriferous region, declares as his conviction, that, *all things considered*, Georgia, as a gold-mining region, offers inducements equal to those of California. We quote his remarks on this point, as they are both full and interesting. He says:

"But you must remember that this is not the best point that is offered by our North Georgia mines. You see it is not the quantity of gold that makes a section valuable to miners. It is the facility with which the ore is mined; it is the ease with which it can be sent to market; it is the cheapness of labor; it is the nearness of timber and water courses; it is the healthfulness of the climate and the facility with which provisions may be procured. In all these points Georgia excels. A ton of ore in the Black Hills. of twice the richness, is not worth as much as a ton of ore in Georgia. A mine of enormous richness is of little value if it is in the heart of an impenetrable or dangerous or malarious region. Lumps of gold might exist at the north pole without being of any practical value. There are scientists who believe that great masses of this precious metal are to be found at the centre of the earth. Of what account is it, however, to us?

"Now, the gold of North Georgia is in a perfectly accessible region. It is penetrated by first-class railways, and by short and reliable hack lines. Every part of it is civilized, and convenient to cities. And better 'than all, the gold lies near to the surface, and is easily reached by the miner. The timber needed to run the furnaces is right at hand, and procurable cheap. The climate is the best in the world, and is a famous resort for invalids. The water courses that pour down the hills give the best possible power,

It is necessary to transport only a short distance, while in California it is frequently carried fifty and one hundred miles. Labor is cheap and easily procurable. In fact, all the elements of cheap working for gold appear to be united in this section.

"The greatest advantage, however, is in the fact that most of the ore in North Georgia is partially decomposed, and is worked with great facility. Where you would have to blast the quartz in California, you can work it with a pick, or even a shovel. Consequently, ore that is much poorer than the California ore can be mined here at a profit, while there it would involve a loss. It does look as if nature had conspired to put the enormous amount of gold in North Georgia in the hands of the miner.

"Besides the above advantages, it is very rich—as rich as any ore to be found anywhere."

Such is the testimony of an intelligent and disinterested officer of the government, who owns not a foot of our gold territory, nor a share in our mines.

The gold belt of Georgia is about one hundred miles in breadth, with barren intervals here and there. It lies northeast and southwest across the entire northern and part of the eastern section of the State, and loses itself in the eastern portion of Alabama. It extends through a large number of counties. It has been found as low as Columbia county, in the eastern portion of Middle Georgia, and as far north and west as Fannin county, which borders on the State of Tennessee. But few mines have been developed in Columbia and Lincoln counties, but they are claimed to be among the richest in the State. A vein near Goshen, in the latter county, is said to be yielding at the present time, $1,000 per month at a cost of but $115. That portion of intermediate territory which is barren of gold, is comparatively small, being much less than one-half of the whole. While many very rich and profitable mines have been opened in the lower portion of the belt, the greater proportion of the mining has been done in the northern or mountainous section, especially in the counties of Lumpkin, White, Union, Dawson and Cherokee.

POPULATION.

The population of Georgia, as stated in the census of 1870—the last taken—numbers 1,184,109. Of these 637,926 are white, and 595,192 black and mulatto. The white population of the coast country are the decendants of original settlers from England Scotland and the German speaking nations of Europe, with a considerable admixture of families from the Northern States of the American Union. Middle Georgia was settled chiefly by immigrants from Maryland, Virginia and the Carolinas, while in Upper Georgia, whose settlement is of a very recent date, the inhabitants came chiefly from Tennessee and North and South Carolina.

HEALTH.

The idea obtains, among those who have not taken the trouble to inform themselves on the subject, that Georgia, because she is a Southern State, has an unwholesome atmosphere, making health insecure within her borders. This objection we have somewhat anticipated in our remarks on climate. There could be no greater error, as a comparison of vital statistics will abundantly show. The health of Georgia will average quite as well as that of any State in the Union. Our citizens of Northern nativity will sustain us in this declaration. The great diversity of climate, resulting from a gradual elevation from the seacoast to the Piedmont country, amounting to from 1,600 to 1,800 feet, precludes the idea of a malarious country. In the low country, immediately along the lines of rivers and swamps, it is conceded that the atmosphere is impure, and that such districts are subject to remittent and intermittent fevers during the summer and fall months ; these, however, are generally of a mild type, and readily yield to proper medical treatment. But, owing to the favorable face of the country in this section of the State, being plentifully supplied with hills and highlands, even those who cultivate the swamps and river bottoms can fix their residences in the vicinity, where they will not be exposed to their malarial influences. And these influences are being rapidly annihilated year after year, by draining and reducing to dry culture the swamps, which, when thus reclaimed become both harmless and among the most productive lands in the State. There are large districts that were considered next to uninhabitable thirty years ago from this cause, but which are now filled with a thriving population, who find no difficulty in residing in them the year round.

These latter remarks apply exclusively to the Southern division of the State ; in Middle and Upper Georgia, the atmosphere is as pure and wholesome, and the health of the inhabitants as perfect and uninterrupted, as on any portion of the continent. Indeed, these sections, especially the latter, are favorite resorts of invalids and pleasure-seekers during the summer and early fall months, from all parts of the South; while the pine lands of Southern Georgia are annually visited in winter by large numbers from the Northern States suffering from pulmonary affections, rheumatism, etc. Consumption is a disease almost unknown in Georgia, except when imported from other States. In Middle and Northern Georgia are to be found all our medicinal springs and watering places, and thousands annually throng to them in search of health or recreation. Under a theory that has obtained much favor among medical men of late years, that weak or diseased lungs require light and pure, rather than warm air, the direction of pulmonary invalids has been considerably changed from the semi-tropical to the Piedmont region, during the winter months. The town of Marietta, in Cobb county, 1,132 feet above the sea, has for years been resorted to by this class of invalids, while the hotel at Mt. Airy, in Habersham county, 1,588 feet above the sea, was well patronized during the past winter by consumptives, and with happy results.

For the information of those who object to Georgia on the score of latitude and its supposed unhealthiness, we would institute a single, but most striking comparison : The State of Michigan, in the extreme Northern portion of the Union, and bordering on Canada, with an atmosphere purified by perpetual breezes from the surrounding lakes, is esteemed to be one of the healthiest States in the Union. Her population and that of Georgia, according to the last census, approximate so closely that there is a difference of but just *fifty* souls, and the vital statistics of the two States, respectively, show that their death rates are about the same. It is difficult to answer such facts and figures as these, and ignorance and prejudice must give way to truth founded on actual experience.

EDUCATION.

Every man who has a proper regard for the welfare of his posterity, in selecting a home for himself and family, will be influenced, in a large measure, by the facilities which it offers for the education of his children. In this respect, also, Georgia presents peculiar advantages, such as are enjoyed to a very limited extent in newly-settled countries, and superior, in all respects to those of the other Southern States of the Union. To elaborate her system would require a volume, and we shall only glance at its various features.

THE UNIVERSITY OF GEORGIA, located at Athens, in Clark county, was incorporated and endowed by a donation of public lands, 40,000 acres, in the year 1784, or soon after the province was organized as a State. It has a permanent endowment of $370,-552.17. It has five Educational Departments, thirteen professors, and over two hundred students. The Curriculum of studies is thorough. It admits "fifty meritorious young men of limited means," and "young men who design to enter the ministry, of any religious denomination," free of charge for tuition. The college libraries contain about 20,000 volumes.

Connected with the University is the State College of Agriculture and the Mchanic Arts, with its Experimental Farm and Workshops. It has three departments, viz : Agriculture, Engineering and Applied Chemistry, each with a regular course. The tuition in this school is made free to as many young men of the State as there are representatives (175) and senators (44) in the Legislature, and the students of both the University proper and the Agricultural and Mechanical Schools have, each, free admisson to the instruction given in the other.

There are, also, a Law School, at Athens, and a Medical School at Augusta, connected with the State University.

The North Georgia Agricultural College, at Dahlonega, Lumpkin county, at which near three hundred students are now being educated free of charge, is also attached to the State University and governed by the same board of trustees. It is proposed to establish a similar school at a point more convenient than either Athens or Dahlonega to pupils residing in the southern half of the State, and it will no doubt be carried into effect at some future day. Military tactics are taught both at Athens and Dahlonega as a part of the regular course, and competent professors are provided in that department.

MERCER UNIVERSITY is located at Macon, Bibb county, was established by the Baptist church, and is wholly under the control of that denomination of Christians. It has nine professors, and the course of instruction is thorough. Attached to it are a Law and a Theological Department, at Macon, and Preparatory schools at Penfield, in Green county, and at Dalton, in Whitfield county. Its libraries, contain about 12,000 volumes ; the buildings and grounds cost $150,000 ; endowment, $160,000. The institution enjoys a large patronage, a considerable portion of which is received from other denominations.

EMORY COLLEGE, at Oxford, Newton county, belongs to the Methodist Episcopal Church, South, and is the joint property of the North Georgia, South Georgia, and Florida Conferences. Like the other colleges of the State, it is well supplied with apparatus has a good library, and is well patronized.

PIO NONO COLLEGE, at Macon, as its name imports, is a Roman Catholic institution, but recently established. It is well supported by our citizens of that religious faith, and bids fair to rank well among Georgia's institutions of learning.

To the above may be added the *Atlanta University*, established by northern donations for the education of the blacks, male and female, and supported, in part, by appropriations from the State Treasury. Its course of instruction, classical and mathematical, is very thorough. It has 4 professors, 9 teachers, a good library, and the classes of 1877-78 numbered, in the aggregate—

FEMALE COLLEGES.—For the education of females in the higher branches, we have a number of colleges, well distributed over the State. We mention the Wesleyan Female College, at Macon, the first female college ever established in Georgia; Cherokee Baptist Female College, at Rome; Southern Masonic Female College, at Covington; Rome Female College, at Rome; Dalton Female College, at Dalton; Houston Female College, at Perry; Conyers Female College; Young Female College at Thomasville; Andrew Female College, at Cuthbert; Monroe Female College, at Forsyth; Gordon Institute, at Barnesville; Gainesville College, at Gainesville; Le Vert Female College, at Talbotton; La Grange Female College and Southern Female College, at La Grange; Furlow Masonic Female College, at Americus, and West Point Female College. Nearly all these institutions are flourishing, and turning out annually, in the aggregate, large numbers of well-educated and well-mannered young women to adorn and elevate society.

Besides these, there are large numbers of high schools, both male and female, very many of them ranking among the bes institutions of learning in the South.

Nor is Georgia unmindful of her unfortunate children whom nature has stinted in the bestowment of her gifts; nor has she been niggardly in providing for their wants in this respect, and in making them useful to themselves and to others. Large and costly edifices have been erected by the State for the care and education of the blind, and of the deaf and dumb—for the former at Macon, and for the latter at Cave Spring, in Floyd county. Both these unfortunate classes are taught not only in the learning of the schools, but also those useful occupations which render them measurably independent.

PUBLIC SCHOOL SYSTEM.

The Common Schools of Georgia form, by far the most interesting feature of her educational system. Recognizing the great moral and political truth that intelligence and virtue form the basis of all good government, the people of Georgia have inserted in their Constitution, or fundamental law, a provision declaring that "there shall be a thorough system of common schools for the education of children," which "shall be free to all the children of the State," the expenses of which "shall be provided for by taxation, or otherwise." In accordance with this constitutional provision, the necessary laws have been passed, and the system referred to is now in successful and beneficent operation, the whites and the blacks being educated in separate schools. The State appropriates annually, for the support of these free schools, about $300,000, and this sum is supplemented each year by local, city and county appropriations to the amount of between $140,000 and $150,000. The number of pupils in actual attendance on these shools last year (1877), was in round numbers, 191,000, of whom 127,000 were whites and 64,000 blacks. The progressive interest in, and usefulness of, the system are illustrated by the statistics of attendance from year to year. In 1871, but seven years ago, when it was put in operation, the number of children taught was but 49,578—42,914 whites and 6,664 blacks. In 1874 the number had increased to 145,541, in 1876, to 179,405; and in 1877, to upwards of 190,100.

The Common School organization extends to every county in the State, and includes every district or subdivision of the counties where the population is sufficiently numerous to admit of a school; so that there is scarcely a child in Georgia who is not within reach of a school where a good education can be obtained free of expense.

In fine, it may be said with truth that, as respects educational facilities and their adaptation to the public wants, the State of Georgia is in advance of all her sister Southern States; while, in this respect, she is progressing year after year, and will soon stand side by side with the older and more favored commonwealths of the North.

RELIGION.

The laws of Georgia guarantee to the citizen perfect freedom of religious opinion and worship, and there is no political or civil disqualification on account of religious belief. Every denomination is not only tolerated, but protected, in the free enjoyment of faith and worship. As a necessary consequence, there is a complete seperation of Church and State, both by law and practically. Each moves in its appropriate sphere, and neither is allowed to encroach on the other.

GOVERNMENT OF GEORGIA.

The government of Georgia, in common with that of all the States of the American Union, is a Representative Democracy. All officers are chosen directly by the people, or by persons to whom the people, from motives of public policy or convenience, have delegated the power of election.

QUALIFICATION OF VOTERS.—The Constitution of Georgia provides that every male citizen of the United States (except idiots, lunatics, and persons convicted, in any court of competent jurisdiction, of treason against the State, embezzlement of public funds, malfeasance in office, bribery, larceny, or of any crime punishable by imprisonment in the penitentiary), who is twenty-one years of age, who shall have resided in this State one year next preceding the election, and six months in the county in which he offers to vote, and who shall have paid all taxes that have been legally required of him, and which he has had an opportunity of paying, except for the year of the election, shall be deemed an elector, or person qualified to vote at all general elections.

NATURALIZATION.

The acts of Congress provide that an alien may become a citizen of the United States on the following conditions:

1. He shall declare on oath, before a Circuit or District Court of the United States, or a District or Supreme Court of the Territories, or a court of record in any of the States having common law jurisdiction and a seal and clerk, two years, at least, prior to his admission, that it is *bona fide* his intention to become a citizen of the United States, and to renounce forever all allegiance and fidelity to any foreign prince, potentate, state or sovereignty, and, particularly, by name, to the prince, potentate, state or sovereignty of which the alien may be at the time a citizen or subject.

2. At the time of making this application, he must take an oath before the same court to support the Constitution of the United States, and that he entirely renounces and abjures all allegiance and fidelity to any foreign prince, potentate, etc.

3. At the time of admission he must prove, to the satisfaction of the court, by testimony other than his own, that he has resided in the United States five years at least; that during that time he has maintained a good moral character, and that he is attached to the principles of the Constitution of the United States, and well disposed to the good order and preservation of the same. He must also renounce any hereditary title, or order of nobility, that he may have borne, if any, previous to his admission to citizenship.

4. If the alien be under twenty-one years of age, and has resided in the United States three years previous to his arrival at that age, if he subsequently apply for admission, the three years of his minority will be counted in estimating his five years of residence, and he will be allowed to make the foregoing declarations and oath at the time of his admission.

5. The minor children, or those under twenty-one years of age, of persons who have been duly naturalized, if dwelling in the United States, are held and considered as citizens thereof.

6. By special act of congress, passed July 17, 1862, any alien of the age of twenty-one years, and upwards, who has enlisted, or may enlist, in the armies of the United States, either the regular,

or the volunteer forces, and has been, or may be hereafter, honorably discharged, shall be admitted to citizenship upon his petition without any previous declaration of his intention, and upon proof of only one year's residence in the United States previous to his application to become a citizens, of his good moral character, and that such person has been honorably discharged from the service of the United States.

7. Seamen who have served three years on any merchant vessel of the United States, after making a declaration of their intention, shall be entitled to become citizens upon application, and the production of a certificate of discharge and good conduct during that time, together with a certificate of their declaration of intention to become citizens.

Aliens, the subjects of governments at peace with the United States and this State, so long as their governments remain at peace, shall be entitled to all the rights of citizens of other States resident in this State, and shall have the privilege of purchasing, holding, and conveying real estate in this State.

This gives to aliens or unnaturalized subjects of foreign governments, whether resident or not, so long as their governments continue at peace with the United States and this State, all rights enjoyed by citizens of this State, except the right to vote and hold office, and to perform such civil functions as are confined by law to citizens of this State.

LIST OF NEWSPAPERS, ETC., PUBLISHED IN GEORGIA.

NAME.		ADDRESS.
Berrien County News	(weekly)	Alapaha, Berrien county
Advertiser	(weekly)	Albany.
News	(weekly)	"
Sumter Republican	(semi-weekly)	Americus.
Recorder	(weekly)	"
Southern Watchman	(weekly)	Athens.
Southern Cultivator	(monthly)	"
Southern Banner	(weekly)	"
Weekly Chronicle	(weekly)	"
Atlanta Constitution	(daily)	Atlanta.
Evening Post	(daily)	"
Evening Dispatch	(daily)	"
Globe	(weekly)	"
Medical and Surgical Journal	(monthly)	"
Republican	(weekly)	"
Boys and Girls of the South	(semi-monthly)	"
Christian Index	(weekly)	"
Georgia Templar	(weekly)	"
Methodist Advocate	(weekly)	"
Southern Enterprise	(monthly)	"
Southern Medical Record	(monthly)	"
Southern Planter and Grange	(weekly)	"
Sunny South	(weekly)	"
Georgia Clinical Record	(monthly)	"
Jewish South	(weekly)	"
Sunday Gazette	(weekly)	"
Sunday Phonograph	(weekly)	"
Southern Real Estate Gazette	(monthly)	"
Commercial Reporter	(monthly)	"
Kennesaw Route Gazette	(monthly)	"
Piedmont Air-Line HeadLight	(monthly)	"
Chronicle & Constitutionalist	(daily)	Augusta.
Evening News	(daily)	"
Democrat	(weekly)	Bainbridge.
Gazette	(weekly)	Barnesville.
News	(weekly)	Blackshear.
Early County News	(weekly)	Blakely.
Seaport Appeal	(weekly)	Brunswick.
Advertiser	(weekly)	"
Argus	(weekly)	Buena Vista.
Herald	(weekly)	Butler.

Times	(weekly)	Calhoun.
Cherokee Georgian	(weekly)	Canton.
Franklin County Register	(weekly)	Carnesville.
Carroll County Times	(weekly)	Carrolton.
Express	(weekly)	Cartersville.
Free Press	(weekly)	"
Congregational Methodist	(weekly)	Cave Spring.
Express	(weekly)	Cedartown.
Record	(weekly)	"
Blue Ridge Echo	(weekly)	Cleveland.
Enquirer-Sun	(daily)	Columbus.
Times	(daily)	"
Courier	(weekly)	Conyers.
Examiner	(weekly)	"
Cochran Enterprise	(weekly)	Cochran.
Georgia Enterprise	(weekly)	Covington.
Star	(weekly)	"
Democrat	(weekly)	Crawfordville
Baptist Banner	(weekly)	Cumming.
Clarion	(weekly)	"
Appeal	(weekly)	Cuthbert.
True Southron	(weekly)	"
Mountain Signal	(weekly)	Dahlonega.
Enterprise	(weekly)	Dalton.
North Georgia Citizen	(weekly)	" .
Independent Headlight	(weekly)	"
Timber Gazette	(weekly)	Darien.
Weekly Journal	(weekly)	Dawson.
DeKalb County News	(weekly)	Decatur.
Gazette	(weekly)	Dublin.
Star	(weekly)	Douglasville.
Okefenokean	(weekly)	Du Pont.
Times	(weekly)	Eastman,
Broad Axe and Itemizer	(weekly)	Eatonton.
Gazette	(weekly)	Elberton.
Courier	(weekly)	Ellijay.
Star	(weekly)	Fairburn.
Monroe Advertiser	(weekly)	Forsyth.
Fort Gaines Tribune	(weekly)	Fort Gaines.
Mirror	(weekly)	Fort Valley.
Advertiser	(weekly)	"
Eagle	(weekly)	Gainesville.
North Georgia Argus	(weekly)	"
Southron	(weekly)	"

Home Journal........................(weekly)....................Greensboro.
Herald...(weekly)..................... "
Meriwether Co. Vindicator.....(weekly)....................Greenville.
News..(daily).....................Griffin.
Sun..(weekly) "
Georgia Advertiser.................(monthly).................... "
Journal......................................(weekly)....................Hamilton.
Henry County Weekly...........(weekly)....................Hampton.
Sun..(weekly)....................Hartwell.
Dispatch............................(weekly)....................Hawkinsville
Gazette......................................(weekly)....................Hinesville.
Southerner and Appeal...........(weekly)....................Irwinton.
Butler County Argus.............(weekly)....................Jackson.
Forest News............................(weekly)....................Jefferson.
Sentinel....................................(weekly)....................Jessup.
News..(weekly)....................Jonesboro.
Walker County Messenger......(weekly)....................La Fayette.
Reporter....................................(weekly)....................La Grange.
Gwinnett Herald....................(weekly)....................Lawrenceville
Oglethorpe Echo.....................(weekly)....................Lexington.
News and Farmer..................(weekly)....................Louisville.
Independent.............................(weekly)....................Lumpkin.
South Georgian........................(weekly)....................McVille.
Kind Words.............................(weekly)....................Macon.
Baptist Gem.............................(weekly).................... "
Central Georgia Weekly.........(weekly).................... "
Telegraph and Messenger........(daily).................... "
Wesleyan Christian Advocate.(weekly).................... "
Madisonian..............................(weekly)....................Madison.
Journal......................................(weekly)....................Marietta.
Field and Fireside..................(weekly).................... "
Union and Recorder...............(weekly)....................Milledgevile.
Montezuma Weekly.................(weekly)....................Montezuma.
Herald......................................(weekly)....................Newnan.
Leader......................................(weekly).................... "
Pioneer....................................(weekly)....................Pearson.
Home Journal..........................(weekly)....................Perry.
Reporter....................................(weekly)....................Quitman.
Free Press................................(weekly).................... "
Catoosa Courier.......................(weekly)....................Ringgold.
Dade County Gazette..............(weekly)....................Rising Fawn.
Bulletin....................................(weekly)....................Rome.
Rome Daily..............................(daily).................... "
Courier....................................(weekly).................... "

Tribune	(weekly)	Rome.
Courier	(weekly)	Sandersville.
Herald and Georgian	(weekly)	"
Abend Zeitung	(weekly)	Savannah.
Morning News	(daily)	"
Sunday Telegram	(weekly)	"
Southern Farmer's Monthly	(monthly)	"
Southern Musical Journal	(monthly)	"
Farm and Home	(weekly)	Senoia.
Walton County Vidette	(weekly)	Social Circle.
Times and Planter	(weekly)	Sparta.
Ishmaelite	(weekly)	"
Herald	(weekly)	Swainsboro.
Summerville Gazette	(weekly)	Summerville.
Telephone	(weekly)	Sylvania:
Standard	(weekly)	Talbotton.
Georgia Register	(weekly)	"
Upson Enterprise	(weekly)	Thomaston.
Southern Enterprise	(weekly)	Thomasville.
Times	(weekly)	"
McDuffie Journal	(weekly)	Thomson.
Herald	(weekly)	Toccoa City.
Times	(weekly)	Valdosta.
Clipper	(weekly)	Warrenton.
Gazette	(weekly)	Washington.
State Line Press	(weekly)	West Point.

RAILROADS IN GEORGIA.

The following is a list of the railroads in this State, together with the length of each within the State lines:

Western & Atlantic, from Atlanta to Chattanooga, Tenn...138 miles
Marietta & North Ga., from Marietta to Canton............. 24 "
Rome Branch, from Kingston to Rome........................... 20 "
Cherokee R. R., from Cartersville to Rockmart.............. 23 "
A. & R. Air-Line, from Atlanta to Charlotte—in Ga......100 "
Northeastern, from Athens to Lula City...................... 40 "
Elberton Air-line, from Elberton to Toccoa City............. 51 "
Georgia, from Augusta to Atlanta..............................171 "
Washington Branch, from Barnett to Washington.......... 18 "
Athens Branch, from Union Point to Athens................. 39 "
Savannah & Augusta, from Augusta to Millen............... 53 "
Georgia Central, from Savannah to Atlanta..................295 "
Sandersville Branch, from Tennille to Sandersville......... 3 "
Eatonton Branch, from Gordon to Eatonton................... 39 "

Thomaston Branch, from Barnesville to Thomaston........ 16 miles
Savannah, Griffin and N. Ala., from Griffin to Carrollton 60 "
Savannah & Skidaway, from Savannah to Isle of Hope... 9 "
Montgomery Branch, from Isle of Hope to Montgomery... 4 "
Atlantic & Gulf, from Savannah to Bainbridge.............237 "
Live Oak Branch, from Lawton to Live Oak, Fla............ 48 "
Albany Branch, from Thomasville to Albany.................. 60 "
Macon & Augusta, from Macon to Camak, Ga. R. R........ 74 "
Macon & Brunswick, from Macon to Brunswick.............186 "
Hawkinsville Branch, from Cochran to Hawkinsville...... 10 "
Brunswick & Albany, from Brunswick to Albany...........172 "
Southwestern, from Macon to Eufaula, Ala.....................140 "
Muscogee Branch, from Fort Valley to Columbus............ 71 "
Perry Branch, from Fort Valley to Perry....................... 11 "
Albany Branch, from Smithville to Albany................... 23½ "
Arlington Branch, from Albany to Arlington.................. 35¾ "
Fort Gaines Branch, from Cuthbert to Fort Gaines........ 22 "
North & South, from Columbus to Kingston................... 20 "
Selma, Rome & Dalton, from Dalton to Selma, Ala.—in Ga. 67 "
Atlanta & West Point, from Atladta to West Point........ 86¾ "
East Tennessee, from Dalton to Bristol, Va.—in Ga......... 18 "
Chattanooga & Alabama, from Chattanooga to Selma,
    Ala.—in Georgia... 25 "
Dodge's R. R., from Eastman, Dodge co., to Ocmulgee R.
    completed... 10 "

PART II.

SECTIONAL DIVISIONS.

SHOWING THE DISTINCTIVE FEATURES OF THE SEVERAL POR-
TIONS OF GEORGIA, ARRANGED WITH A VIEW TO A MORE
INTELLIGIBLE PRESENTATION, TOGETHER WITH LETTERS
RECEIVED FROM ACTUAL SETTLERS FROM OTHER STATES OF
THE UNION AND FOREIGN COUNTRIES.

The large area covered by the State, and the peculiar conjunc-
ture of geographical and topographical features, aided by the disposition of geological strata, have resulted in a great diversity of
climate, soils and productions—greater than in any State of the
Union.

This diversity has made it desirable to divide the whole area
into five sections, by lines, which, to some extent, are indicated
by the changes in topographical features and geological formation.

These sections are described separately, and immediately following the description will be found copies of letters received from
Northern and foreign born citizens who have settled in the State
(with few exceptions) since 1865. These letters were in answer to
the following circular:

Special Circular No. 67.]

STATE OF GEORGIA,
DEPARTMENT OF AGRICULTURE,

ATLANTA, April 25, 1879.

DEAR SIR—

In response to the enclosed circular, No. 64, your name and address has been furnished me by one of my crop correspondents in
your county. As intimated in that circular, my object is to pre-
pare a pamphlet which shall give, from the stand-point of actual
settlers, a view of the natural resources of soil and climate of Georgia, the moral and social condition of the people, their disposition
towards immigrants, and the social position which may be accorded to such immigrants, as judged from your own personal experience and observation.

The pamphlet will be made up chiefly of short statements, over
the name and address of the persons who may respond to this re-

quest, and a large number will be printed for free distribution in the Northern and Western States of the Union, and in foreign countries, with a view to giving emigrants reliable and accurate information of our climate, soil and resources, from the stand-point of actual settlers, and to disabuse their minds of prejudice.

I will be obliged, therefore, if you will give, on this sheet, such a statement—based on your experience and observation—as may serve the purpose in view, as soon as convenient, and mail to this office.   Very respectfully,

THOMAS P. JANES,

Commissioner of Agriculture.

Let the remarks which follow embrace the following: 1. Your native country. 2. The year of your settlement in Georgia. 3. Your business or profession. 4. Inducements presented for those of your own or other professions. 5. Climate. 6. Soil. 7. Productions. 8. Health. 9. Condition of society. 10. Safety to life and property. 11. Taxes. 12. Feeling manifested towards, and social treatment of, immigrants. 13. Prices and profits of land compared with other States or countries; and such other points as may may occur to you as proper and relevant.

Here sign your name..

Your postoffice..

In response to this circular, replies were received from upwards of fifty counties, representing every section of the State. Excepting some slight verbal changes, not affecting the substance, they are printed as received, with the name and post-office address of each, together with the names of other citizens, of the same class, from whom similar letters were received but not published—for want of space.

The facts represented of any one county, are, in the main, applicable to the adjoining counties, from which no letters appear. In some counties there are no settlers of the class to which the circular was addressed; in others their was either a failure on the part of regular correspondents of the DEPARTMENT to furnish names, or neglect on the part of those to whom the foregoing circular was sent.

NORTH GEORGIA.   .

This section embraces all that portion of the state lying north of the tier of counties in which Clarke, Fulton and Carroll may be considered objective points, and includes thirty-three counties in all. For convenience it is sometimes divided, as in the MANUAL

OF GEORGIA, into two sub-sections—Northeast and Northwest Georgia.

NORTHEAST GEORGIA.—This region comprises the following counties :

Banks,	Dawson,	Fannin,	Forsyth,
Franklin,	Gilmer,	Gwinnett,	Habersham,
Hall,	Hart,	Jackson,	Lumpkin,
Madison,	Milton,	Pickens,	Rabun,
Towns,	Union	White.	

It is that part of the State which possesses the greatest elevation, the average being 1,500 feet above the level of the sea, while there are peaks which rise to an elevation of near 5,000 feet. The region is metamorphic, or composed of rocks changed from their original condition by heat and pressure. The geological formations are granite, gneiss, mica and horn-blende schists : soils red and gray, resting on a basis of firm clay, usually red but sometimes yellow, white and blue mixed with gravel, the latter chiefly on lowlands. The clay, or subsoil, is usually found from four to six inches below the surface on uplands, from one to two feet in the valleys, and from two to six feet in river bottoms. The original forest growth is chiefly red, black, post and white oaks; chestnut, black-jack, hickory, short-leaf and spruce pine, cedar, dogwood, black-gum, walnut, with poplar, ash, elm, sycamore, birch, sweet-gum and white-oak on the lowlands. This is the great auriferous region of the State, the net yield of gold being equal to that of any section of the Union, California not excepted. Copper, lead, magnetic iron ore, mica, asbestus, marble, ruby, serpentine, corundum are also found in considerable quantities, and may be mined with profit.

The lands are generally rich and productive, the yield depending wholly on the skill used in their cultivation. The staple field products are Indian corn, wheat, oats, rye, barley, clover, the various grasses and sorghum cane, while in the Southern portion of the division cotton is grown to a conserable extent. The average yield per acre, under fair cultivation, is : corn, 20 bushels : wheat, 15 bushels ; oats, 25 bushels ; rye, 8 bushels ; barley, 25 bushels ; hay, from 2 to 3 tons ; sorghum syrup, 75 gallons : cotton, 400 pounds in the seed. Under high culture, two, three and sometimes four times this production is realized. Tobacco, buckwheat and German millet can also be grown with great success. The planting and harvest times of the division are as follows : corn, planted 15th March to 15th May, gathered in fall months; wheat and other small grain, sown October, harvested in June and July; cotton, planted 15th April to 15th May, gathered in fall months : sorghum, planted in April, cut in August. A very large proportion of the laborers, both farm and mine, are white; wages of former, $8 to $10 per month; of latter 75 cents to $1 per day; ordinary mechanics, $1 to $2 per day, according to skill.

The fruits best adapted to the section are the apple, cherry, pear, grape, plum, in all its varieties, peach, gooseberry, raspberry, strawberry—the last named producing equally well in all parts of the State with like cultivation. Almost every variety of vegetables attain to great perfection.

The climate is unsurpassed on the continent for comfort and salubrity during nine months of the year. The mean temperature in summer is 70° Fahrenheit, in winter 35°; highest temperature 90°, lowest 8°—periods of greater heat and cold being exceptional. Snow falls usually from two to three times during the winter season, especially in the northernmost counties, to a depth varying from two inches to six inches. In the Southern tier of counties, there are occasional winters without a fall of snow.

Springs and running streams abound in all parts of the district; water powers unsurpassed; spring and well water freestone, and not excelled in any country. Mineral springs—sulphur or chalybeate—abound in nearly all the counties of the district. That portion of it—the eastern—to which railroad transportation has been opened, is annually visited by thousands, many of whom spend the entire summer and part of autumn at its watering places and pleasant villages. It may be said of this, and indeed of all other sections of the State, that the people are anxious for new settlers, and are ready to give a cordial welcome to honest and industrious immigrants from all countries, including our own. Lands can be bought at low prices and on favorable terms, as regards the payments—in the mountains from $1 to $5 per acre, and in the valleys and lower portions of the district from $5 to $10 per acre. The average price of farm stock varies but little in the State, and may be stated as follows: milch cows, $15 to $20; sheep, $1.50 to $2; brood sows, $5 to $8; horses and mules, $75 to $100.

NORTHWEST GEORGIA.—The following counties are included in this sub-section:

Bartow,	Catoosa,	Chattooga,	Cherokee,
Cobb,	Dade,	Floyd,	Gordon,
Haralson,	Murray,	Paulding,	Polk,
Walker,	Whitfield.		

Northwest Georgia extends from the Cohutta Mountains and Chattahoochee Ridge to the eastern boundary of Alabama. It differs in several important respects from the Northeastern division. It is less mountainous, and, consequently, a greater portion of its area is susceptible of cultivation. Its average elevation above the sea is only 750 feet, or about 50 per cent. less than that of Northeast Georgia. Its geological ages are Silurian, Devonian (so called from their identity with those of Wales and Devonshire, and, in the extreme northwest, carboniferous. The characteristic minerals are limestone, slate, iron ores, coal, manganese, sandstone, baryta, some gold, all of which, except the last, are found in great quantities. Several valuable veins and gravelly deposits of gold have been developed and worked with handsome returns.

The immense coal beds described in the chapter on minerals lie the northwestern counties of this division, to-wit: Dade, Walker and Chattooga. The supply seems to be inexhaustible. The mines are reached by railroads which connect with main trunks, and in the immediate vicinity are immense deposits of best iron ore.

The soils are calcerous and argillaceous; clay red and yellow. In all other respects our description of the natural conditions and capabilities of Northeast Georgia will apply to this division, with the single exception of temperature, the difference in elevation being accompanied by the usual variations of heat and cold. The productions are, in all respects, the same.

In one or two respects, this division enjoys peculiar advantages over its eastern neighbor. It has not only a larger area of tillable land, but a much greater proportion of valley and river bottom. Its facilities for transportation are also greater, the Western and Atlantic Railroad traversing its centre from the northern to the southern boundary, while tributary roads supply a good portion of the country to the right and left of the main line.

The whole of North Georgia is admirably adapted to stock-raising. The mountains afford abundant pasturage for cattle, sheep, hogs, goats, etc., which are required to be fed only a few months in the year, while the grains and grasses are produced in the greatest abundance for that purpose.

LETTERS FROM ACTUAL SETTLERS.

BANKS COUNTY.

I was born in Northern Ohio; went from there to North Carolina in 1873, and came to Georgia in 1874. I am a physician, and have been well patronized and well treated since my residence here. I believe I am the only Northern man now residing in Banks county who came since 1865. I find the climate delightful and healthy; no malarial diseases excellent freestone water. People live here to an extreme old age. One man has died since my residence here, aged 114 years, and one woman, his wife, at 108; also a colored woman at the age of 106 years, two others, said to be about 100, and several are now living nearly 100.

The soil is well adapted to corn, wheat, oats and cotton. The heat in summer is not so oppressive as at the North, and the winters are delightful. The inhabitants, in the main, are honest, industrious and of temperate habits. Education is at a low ebb, but efforts are being made for more and better schools. A man's life and property are as

3

safe here as in any part of the United States. Doors are seldom locked, and larceny is seldom heard of. I have never felt that I was slighted or ostracized for being a yankee, but I believe in many instances I have been treated with more courtesy because of my nativity, for the purpose of correcting any wrong impression I may have received.

Wild land is held at from $2 to $10 per acre, and improved farms at from $7 to $20. Farming pays as large per cent. on investment as in any part of the United States. Good mechanics, especially blacksmiths, are needed; but most of all, experienced and well qualified teachers, male and female.   THOMAS HAYDEN,
                                          Homer, Banks county, Ga.

BARTOW COUNTY.

I came here from Toronto, Canada, in November, 1875; since, I have been farming in Fulton county, and here in Bartow. The climate is delightful and healthy. In Canada, I had consumption, but have entirely recovered since coming here. The soil is fertile, producing all the grains, cotton, rice, tobacco—everything a man requires to live well. The society is good, taxes low, and life and property as safe here as in Canada. Immigrants are kindly treated—the feeling towards them is most friendly. Land is cheap, and with proper management pays a good profit on the amount invested. Labor is cheap and efficient to those wanting help, and laborers can get employment on farms at remunerative rates.   E. MURRAY,
                                          Cartersville, Bartow county, Ga.

COBB COUNTY.

Massachusetts is my native State—as it was the home of my ancestors—and there I learned my trade as a wool manufacturer, the business in which I am now engaged at this place. I think I can say, without fear of contradiction, that this section of Georgia presents many superior advantages over any section of the United States for the manufacture of wool and cotton. 1. There is no section better supplied with unlimited water powers, desirably located. 2. The climate is well adapted to the business; the mercury seldom rising above 92° in the summer, while the nights are cool and invigorating. 3. We can operate for eight months in the year with little or no expense for heating, while the remaining four months cost but little compared with Northern States. 4. A good supply of the raw material can always be secured at home, from first hands, and much of the freights, commissions, and other profits for handling, be saved. 5. The natives here make good operatives. As a general rule, they are intelligent, sober and industrious. In fact, there is nothing in the way of success to the energetic, skillful manufacturer. Much more might be said; but a word to the wise is sufficient—come and see. There are many inducements to immigrants. Society is good; life and property are as safe as in any part of the United States. Referring to my own experience, I came here in 1859—just before the late unfortunate war commenced. I remained until General Sherman passed this point, and then went North, where I staid two years. I then returned to this place (Roswell). where I desire to spend the remainder of my days, as I am well pleased with the country, climate and society. Although I have differed in my political views with most of the people with whom I have associated, yet the most kindly feelings have been manifested towards me, and also to other immigrants to this section. To those wishing to come to this section, let me say to them, they will find a most hearty welcome in our midst, and the advantages of good water powers, climate, soil, health and society not surpassed in any part of our wide domain.

                              J. S. WOOD, President,
                              Roswell, Cobb county, Ga.

I am a native of western New York, and by occupation a farmer. I am well pleased with this country, and consider it unsurpassed in the United States for climate and healthfulness, best of water, good timber, long, good seasons of fruit, cheap lands, low taxes and good markets. The land is susceptible of high improvement.

I have received generous treatment from the most intelligent portion of the people, and with few exceptions, from the common and less informed. A man is safe here as anywhere, from all harm or molestation, if he minds his own business. The people here take offense quicker, and the pistol and knife are more frequently handy than in the North. I do know that this ten dollar land can soon be made worth $40 to $50 by generous treatment. I have done it, and am still doing this. Last season I made 70 bales of cotton from 110 acres—nine-tenths of it old worn land.

I would advise Northern people to bring a few of their old friends for neighbors, as they will enjoy themselves better socially ; old friends being much more dear than new ones, especially since the customs of the people North and South are so different.

J. I. CHAMBERLAIN, Marietta, Ga.

[Letters were also received from Mr. Anthony Van Wick, banker (from New York); postoffice, Marietta; Wm. Hunter (from Scotland) ; postoffice, Roswell, and F. A. E. Schieling, (from Germany) ; postoffice, Marietta. Their experience, in the main, agrees with the foregoing statements.]

DADE COUNTY.

New York is my native State. I am a farmer, and settled here in 1870. The inducements to immigration are many. It is an excellent grazing country, with plenty of cheap uncultivated lands, sufficient for several large colonies. The climate is delightful, and as healthy as the highlands of New York. The soil is a sandy loam, producing well, with moderate fertilizing, all that Ohio produces, and in addition, cotton. There is plenty of good society, and life and property are as secure as in any of the Northern States—even to Northern men. I have received as kind treatment from the native citizens as I ever received in any Northern settlement, and I believe others would receive the same. While the soil is not so rich as in many of the Northern States, the difference is more than made up in the climate, and the price of land is not more than half so great In this county are the table lands of Lookout and Sand Mountains, and on them are thousands of acres of grazing land, well adapted to stock and to fruit growing, besides abundant valley lands, large tracts of which can be bought at a very low price.

R. S. LEAVITT, Smith's P. O., Ga.

I was born in France, and came to Georgia in 1850, following the profession of a miller. The climate is mild, the soil generally good and productive, and health excellent. The society surpasses that of any other State. Life and property are as safe as anywhere. Immigrants are kindly and respectfully treated. Land ranges in price from $2 to $20 per acre. Mountain land especially good for vegetables and fruits of all kinds, and the soil, in general, produces from 10 to 50 bushels of wheat and corn per acre. Mineral products are splendid—iron ore, coal and fire proof clay abundant, and the water everywhere good.

J. H. J. COPUT, Rising Fawn, Ga.

FLOYD COUNTY.

I am from New York; moved to Ohio, where I was reared, and came to Georgia in 1865. I am so well pleased that I shall make it my permanent home. Been farming since 1870, and think this is as good a farming country as there is in the United States, and the business just as profitable. The climate is so even and temperate that even a white man can work in the fields all the year round. Our soil is fertile, and will produce equal to any in the Northern States, and is more easily cultivated than those of the West. I have grown 310 bushels of corn on five acres, and 163 gallons syrup on one acre, both crops being made without any special pains, and without manure. I have had clover 5½ feet in length. The country in this part of Georgia is as healthy as can be found in the world; the society is equal to any in the Union. Very few vagabonds here, and as for tramps, I have not seen one. No State where life and property are safer. The social treatment of immigrants is good—so far as I have heard. I have been here nearly 14 years, and have been treated kindly by all. In 1867 I married one of Georgia's purest and fairest daughters. So, you see, there is no disposition to treat Northern men otherwise than as gentlemen, if they conduct themselves as such—at least such is my experience.

The prices of land run from $2.00 to $50.00 per acre, according to location and proximity to Rome. The profits of farming are equal to the West, and if our farmers were as careful as the Western people, our profits would be greater, as our markets are better. I have traveled over most of the Western States, and found none that is equal to Georgia as a home.   E. M. EASTMAN, Rome, Ga.

My native State is New York. Moved to Michigan in 1834, and to this city (Rome) in 1872, and engaged in my profession of Apiarian. Inducements to apiculture and other branches of industry, good. Climate excellent. Soil and productions fair. Health extremely good. Life and property secure. Taxes moderate. Feelings manifested towards, and social treatment of immigrants, of the "best kind." Prices of land "exceedingly low." No State in the Union affords better or greater inducements to immigrants. During the seven years we have been here we have traveled some in South Carolina, Alabama, Florida, and the greater portion of Georgia. We have attended both State and county fairs; we have formed the acquaintance of many of the leading men of the State, and have ever found them to be a high toned and generous people, ever extending a welcome hand to all who desire a home among them, regardless of the section from which they come. Could all the facts pertaining to the state of things as they exist—the climate, soil, society, a kind and generous people—be made known to the world, the South would ere long receive as great or greater tide of immigration than has ever flowed to the far off West.

One word to my Northern friends, who are so often writing to us. Don't be deceived any longer by erroneous statements. If you prefer a mild climate to one where it is freezing half the year, come South. You will find as kind and generous and orderly a people as can be found anywhere. During our seven years stay here— traveling a good deal too— we have never seen but one altercation between "man and man," and it was only a slight "brush," and they were *Northern men and bankers at that.*
        A. F. MOON, Rome, Ga.

[An interesting letter was also received from Mr. H. B. Zscheck, Rome, Ga., a native of *Posen*, North Germany.]

FORSYTH COUNTY.

I am Kentuckian; settled here in 1865 as farmer. Inducements are as good as could be desired. The climate is mild, the soil mixed, gray and red, and produces well corn, cotton, small grain. Health and society good; life and property safe; taxes low, and all kindness shown to immigrants that could be asked for. Land from $1 to $50 per acre; profits, 25 to 10 per cent. I will say further, that I have never lived among a cleverer people in my life, and it matters not where a man is raised who comes here, he will be treated as if well as a native. They want immigrants.
        AARON SWINNEY, Big Creek P. O., Georgia.

HARALSON COUNTY.

I am a native of northern Ohio; served four years in Union army; came to Rome, Georgia, in 1867; have lived in Meriwether, Troup, Carroll and Haralson counties; bought land in Carroll county in 1870, and commenced farming on a small scale; made money. I am a teacher by profession, and am now engaged in teaching. The inducements for good teachers are such as to induce me to continue. I have now applications from four settlements to teach next year. The climate is moderate—never too hot and seldom extremely cold. The soil is thin in some sections, but capable of a high degree of improvement. All the small grains can be raised with profit. I have never had any

fear of personal violence, and very little difficulty in regard to social privileges, having always received the kindest treatment from a majority of the people. I have never been interferred with on account of politics but once—when living in a Republican settlement, I was somewhat ostracized because I did not vote to suit them. An honest man can get along here as easily as in any State in the Union. I married into one of the best families in the State. I have had considerable opportunities for forming opinions, and will cheerfully write more at large if you desire.   JOHN B. FORSTER,
Tallapoosa, Ga.

LUMPKIN COUNTY.

I was born in Vermont—came to Georgia in 1868. Am a millwright and machinist by trade, and have been engaged in superintending mining operations, and contracting in building stamp and other mills. The inducements offered in Georgia for my trade is far better at the present time than in any section North that I know of. I consider the climate in North Georgia equal in all respects, and superior in many, to any location I was ever in. The soil, with the same treatment, is equal to that of New England or the West. Continual crops of corn or cotton for years, without manure, will wear out any land ; but the soil here produces better than New England soil would with the same treatment. North Georgia can be called an exceedingly healthy section—far ahead of the North, where the changes are so sudden and severe. Society here is chiefly composed of *honest, industrious, hard-working* people—kind-hearted and hospitable as any people I was ever with. I came here soon after the war, and never want to be treated any better than I have been here ; and I firmly believe that any person who comes here with *honest intentions*, and intends to mind his own business, will find a hearty welcome. I have never heard an expression of ill-feeling against Northern people on account of their politics or nativity. In short, I am well pleased with the South, and expect to remain here.   FRANK W. HALL, Dahlonega, Ga.

PAULDING COUNTY.

I was born and reared in Rhode Island, came to Georgia in 1848. I am a millwright by trade, and have always found business plenty at fair prices. The climate is delightful, the water very good, and I think this is as healthy a place as I have ever found. Uplands are fair, bottom lands splendid. Society very good. We have schools and churches, but there is not such a spirit manifested for education as I would like to see. Life and property are as safe here as anywhere. Immigrants will be cordially received and heartily welcomed by our people, as we are glad to see them. There is plenty of land for all who may come, and at prices to suit, ranging from $1.00 to $50.00 per acre. Fair uplands at from $5.00 to $10.00.   G. A. OWEN, Dallas, Ga.

[A very interesting letter was received from Mr. Franklin Parker, Acworth, Ga., who emigrated from Bordeaux, France. He is highly pleased with the country.]

POLK COUNTY.

I came South in 1870 from Blair county, Pennsylvania, and engaged in the iron business. Since 1872 I have been engaged in farming in this valley. This section is one of the most desirable in the South, both for farming and for other professions. The land is well adapted to raising all kinds of produce that can be raised North, in addition to which our people cultivate a large area in cotton. Produce of all kinds finds a ready market, and, owing to the superior quality of cotton raised in this county, it has always commanded a higher price than in the country below. The climate is all that could be desired. The nights are always cool, however warm the day may have been, which is not the case North. Condition of society is excellent. Our people are fully equal to those of the North, both in education and social refinement. I have never felt more secure as to life and property than I do here—never lock my door at night, as I would do if I lived in the North.

Having lived eight years in this part of Georgia, I feel that I am capable of giving a true statement of the feeling towards, and the treatment of, immigrants, and in face of the many unjust and false charges and insinuations which have appeared in partisan newspapers, I affirm that the people here have always gladly welcomed all who have come South for the purpose of making this their future home, and the most cordial and friendly feelings are manifested towards new comers.

Our people are more and more disposed to divide up their large plantations into small farms and place them on the market. Have had several hundred acres placed in my hands for sale. The place I live on contains 800 acres; cost me $15.000, and, although lands have depreciated in saleable value since I bought, I am so much attached to it, so well pleased with the social surroundings, and so confident that lands will increase in value in the near future, that I would not sell for *double* what I gave. The lands here will average one-half bale cotton to the acre. In the North, lands worth $100 per acre produce no more than 30 to 40 bushels of wheat, and there is no reason why our lands should not be made to produce as much. A they would if the small farm system be adopted

M. V. B. AKE, Cedartown, Ga.

[The statements in the foregoing letter are fully sustained by letters from Messrs. J. S. Noyes and A. Huntington, both of *Cedartown*, and natives of Vermont.]

WALKER COUNTY.

Born in New York state; I moved to Illinois and then to Wisconsin, where I resided 25 years. In 1871 came to or near Chattanooga, Tennessee, but not liking the location came to Walker county, where I purchased a farm and now reside.

Georgia presents many inducements to immigrants. 1st. The climate is much milder, the extremes of heat and cold much less than in the North. I have seen as hot days here in summer as in the North, but the winters here are not to be compared with the rigors of the northern winter. 2d. The cheapness of land. A man can buy a piece of land here for a few hundred dollars, and by industry secure a good living. 3d. The climate being so much milder and the winters so much shorter, farmers have much more time to do other work, and it does not require near the outlay to house stock from the weather, nor near so much fodder to feed them during the winter. 4th. The soil varies, as in almost every country, from the rich bottoms to the uplands and ridge lands, and is adapted to a great variety of crops. The leading crops are: cotton, corn, sweet potatoes, tobacco, rice; and very good crops of wheat, rye, and oats are produced. Sorghum yields from 100 to 200 gallons per acre. This is a very healthy county, and the society is good. Safety to life and property secured. The treatment of northern born citizens is as good as they are accustomed to at the North.

There seems to be rather a preference to foreigners and Northern immigrants. Much attention is given to extend the benefits of education to all classes. There are many going to Texas, but many return, and many more would do the same if they had the means to pay their way back. They get there, and often sickness reduces them to the extremity and necessity of a longer stay away from the good old state of Georgia, where they left the prospect of health, wealth and long life.

ALLEN HUBBARD, Villanow, Ga.

I am from Ireland, and settled in Georgia in 1836. I am a farmer by profession. The climate is excellent, healthful, and soil productive. Society is a fair average; people honest, clever and industrious. Nine-tenths of the population are whites. Life and property secure. Immigrants of good character are treated with the utmost respect. I have found it so for 49 years that I have been here. The Southern people are the most hospitable I have ever been among. Lands vary in price from $1.00 to $25.00 per acre, according to quality. Water—pure limestone. Tan-bark abundant. Churches and school-houses numerous.

A. I. LEET, Rock Spring, Ga.

WHITFIELD COUNTY.

In reply to your inquiries we state that our residence in this State is of eight months duration *only*. We do not propose to settle here permanently. We reside in New York State, and though engaged in business here, *must* be in New York one-half the time to attend to business there. We are manufacturers of axe and pick handles. The timber, both hickory and white oak, is of excellent quality, wonderfully abundant, and easily and cheaply obtained. First-class facilities for manufacturing wood-work exist in this and all the adjoining counties. The climate is healthful and delightful, and the people sociable, agreeable and very hospitable. The laws are wise and well and thoroughly administered. Land is exceedingly low and its natural resources very rich. Taxes very light, and expense of living exceedingly small. In nearly all these points of excellence North Georgia is unsurpassed. WHITNEY & BABCOCK, Dalton, Ga.

[Refer also to James Herron, Dalton, Ga., and W. S. Dyer, Trickem, Ga., from both of whom letters have been received.]

MIDDLE GEORGIA.

This section embraces thirty-nine counties, as follows:

Baldwin,	Douglas,	Jones,	Putnam,
Bibb,	Elbert,	Lincoln,	Rockdale,
Butts,	Fayette,	McDuffie,	Spalding,
Campbell,	Fulton,	Meriwether,	Talbot,
Carroll,	Greene,	Monroe,	Taliaferro,
Clarke,	Hancock,	Morgan,	Troup,
Clayton,	Harris,	Newton,	Upson,
Columbia,	Heard,	Oconee,	Walton,
Coweta,	Henry,	Oglethorpe,	Warren,
DeKalb,	Jasper,	Pike,	Wilkes.

It extends across the State from the Savannah river in the east to the Chattahoochee river in the west, and has an area of about 15,000 square miles. Its southern border may be described with tolerable accuracy by a line from Augusta through Macon to Columbus. It is marked by the head of navigation of the principal rivers. The northern border may be described by a line running through Athens and Atlanta. It is about one hundred miles in width. Its average elevation is 750 feet. The entire region is metamorphic, its rocks granite, gneiss, mica, quartzites, hydromica schist, with some limestone and soapstone. These rocks all extend from the northeast to the southwest, and are crossed frequently at right angles by trap dykes. Its chief minerals are gold, copper, lead, asbestus, graphite, chromic iron, serpentine and soapstone. Gold is found in districts wide apart, and has been worked with satisfactory profit in a few localities, more especially in McDuffie, Lincoln, Wilkes and Carroll. Asbestus is also mined to some extent. The original forest growth consists of red, post, Spanish, and white oaks, and blackjack, hickory, short-leaf pine, with some long-leaf on its southern border; poplar, dogwood, elm, chestnut, maple, beech, birch, ash, black locust, sweet and black gums, walnut and some cedar. This division has three varieties of soil—red or clay, gray and gravelly, and light and sandy, the last named being limited in extent, and confined to the long-leaf pine localities on the southern border. The two former possess great productiveness and durability. After the coast country, they were the first settled, and Middle Georgia has continued to be the most populous division of the State. While the lowlands are of the best quality, the uplands are unsurpassed in fertility and luxuriance of forest growth by those of any country. A very large proportion of the lands has suffered temporary exhaustion by injudicious culture which claimed everything from the soil and returned nothing. This ruinous practice is fast giving way to a more enlightened and economical system. It has been ascertained that no soils on the continent are more susceptible of recuperation and respond so bountifully to generous treatment. The abandoned fields, grown up in stunted pines, and for twenty or forty years considered useful only as pasturage, have been restored to cultivation, and are now among the most productive lands of the State. The staple field products are cotton, corn, oats, and wheat, while all the grains and grasses, and even tobacco may be grown successfully. The average yields, with ordinary culture, are: Cotton, 550 pounds, in seed, per acre; corn, 12 bushels; wheat, 8 bushels; oats, 25 bushels; barley, 30 bushels; rye, 8 bushels; sweet potatoes, 100 bushels; field peas with corn, 5 bushels. Ground peas, chufas, pumpkins, and, indeed, almost every field product are successfully cultivated. Very many farmers double the above averages year after year, whilst under high culture the product is multiplied four or five times, as will be seen in the chapter on that subject. About seventy-five per cent. of the farm laborers of this division are negroes, and the average wages are $8 per month and rations. Wages of ordinary mechanics vary from $1.50 to $3.00 per day, according to skill. The planting and harvest periods of leading products are: Cotton, April, September to December; corn, March, October; wheat, October and November, May and early June; other fall grains harvested same time; those sowed in February and March harvested in June. The fruits to which the section is best adapted are the peach, fig, apple, pear, strawberry, raspberry, melons of all kinds. The peach attains here, and in Southwest Georgia, its greatest perfection, and immense quantities are raised for export, both in their natural and dried state; the same may be said of the apple and blackberry, though the latter is a spontaneous growth and yields abundantly in a wild state. Almost every other variety of fruit known in the Southern States thrives well in this division. The table vegetables are all grown successfully, the hardier varieties the year round. The climate is a happy medium between those of Southern and Northern Georgia, and, in healthfulness, equal to that of any part of the world. There is much uniformity of temperature, sudden rises or falls occurring but rarely. The mean annual temperature is 60° to 64°. Snow falls about once in three years, the depth varying from 1½ to 4 inches. Every portion of the division abounds in running streams, while the spring and well waters are excellent. The difference in elevation between the Northern and the Southern portions of the division being from 650 to 700 feet, the water powers are probably unequalled by those of any similar area on the continent. It would be difficult to fix a limit to its manufacturing facilities in this respect. The society is good and the people educated and refined. Immigration is desired, and good lands can be bought on liberal terms at from $4.00 to $10.00 per acre. The mineral springs are few, but for curative powers are unsurpassed in the Union. The Indian Springs, in Butts county, and the Warm and Sulphur Springs, in Meriwether, are famous resorts of invalids, and enjoy a deserved popularity.

LETTERS FROM ACTUAL SETTLERS.

BALDWIN COUNTY.

My native country is Bavaria. Germany. Came to the United States in 1859, and settled in Georgia in 1865. My business is that of a merchant. I find the climate very agreeable, and altogether more desirable than that of Ohio, where I resided at first. The soil is chiefly devoted to cotton, with a fair proportion of cereals; but is capable of producing all that is essential.

Society is in an advanced condition, equal to any, regardless of country or section. Life and property are as safe as anywhere. Laws well administered, and violators find no favor. The feeling towards new comers is cordial, and respectable and law-abiding people will find this a desirable section. My own experience has been agreeable to all reasonable expectations, and I can recommend the people of my adopted State as generous, noble, and hospitable—extending, always, a willing hand to worthy persons. Politics do not run into that fervency as is represented by newspapers, but a man can be what he pleases, so long as he confines himself to the legitimate exercise of his rights.
ADOLPH JOSEPH, Milledgeville, Ga.

BIBB COUNTY.

My native State is New Jersey. Been a resident of this county seven years. After traveling in several of the Southern States, I have settled permanently in Georgia, and feel that I have found the best State in the Union as regards climate, health, productions, etc. Am engaged in manufacturing carriages and wagons, and a general variety business. Find plenty to do. The industrious need never be idle.

The soil of the State is more varied than in any of the 23 States I have traveled in, and is very productive—growing any kind of grain, fruits, or vegetables, except tropical fruits. Many instances of yields of 45 to 50 bushels of wheat per acre ; and it comes into market eight or ten weeks earlier than Northern wheat. Two crops are often made on the same land in one year. There is seldom a day in the year on which the farmer cannot work to advantage. The society is good, and the people clever and obliging and law-abiding—more so than I have ever found in my travels. Good water, plenty of churches and schools. Lands range from 50 cents to $30.00 per acre, according to locality and improvements. Timber is abundant, and portions of the State are rich in gold, iron and coal. I think the time is not far distant when Georgia will be the "boss" State in the Union. All that is wanting is capital and a few industrious settlers.

LEE DAVIS, box 365, Macon, Georgia.

BUTTS COUNTY.

I came to Georgia from New Hampshire, in 1877, and have since been engaged in the practice of medicine. The inducements in this State, to medical men I do not consider flattering, but they can do as well here as elsewhere. The climate is all that could be desired, far superior to that of any of the Northern States. I have traveled extensively and have never found a healthier locality. The soil is generally good, and well adapted to the cultivation of cotton, tobacco, corn, wheat, oats—in fact, everything but tea and coffee. Society is good, schools and churches numerous, taxes exceedingly low. Life and property as safe here as anywhere in the United States. The kindest feelings are manifested towards immigrants, from whatever quarter. Prices of land, five to ten dollars per acre, and where the land is well cultivated, the profits are much greater than at the North.

W. J. TUCKER, M.D., Jackson, Butts county, Ga.

I am a native of Pennsylvania; lived many years in Ohio; came South in 1860, and joined the editorial corps of the *Memphis Appeal*, on which I served, at various places, until the close of the war; settled in Georgia in 1865, as a printer, etc.

Those engaged in my own, or any other honorable occupation, can succeed in Georgia, or any of the Southern States in which I have resided, as surely as in any other portion of the country. The climate of Central Georgia is delightful: the soil is cheap, and productive of almost everything desirable, except the tropical fruits. This location is very healthy, and instances of longevity are numerous.

Society, so far as the white population is concerned, is much the same as in the North and West. We have the same churches, and schools in abundance; but it must be admitted that the public school system has not reached that degree of perfection witnessed in some of the Northern and Western States. In Georgia, an excellent public school system has been introduced, which, fostered by the State, is rapidly commending itself to the people, and approaching a desirable degree of perfection. Academies and colleges are numerous and well supported.

I am confident that life and property are as safe here as anywhere. It has never been my lot to live among a more peaceable, law-abiding people than those of Middle Georgia. The records show that seven-eights of the lawlessness brought to notice in our courts, originates with the colored race.

Taxes low—total of State and county, only one and one-fourth mills on the dollar. The supply of laborers, and especially of skilled mechanics, is insufficient, and imigrants from any quarter will find this a pleasant section, where all the desirable advantages of civilization can be enjoyed, and remunerative results will follow all well directed efforts of the husbandman.

JOHN B. DUMBLE,
Indian Spring, Ga.

CAMPBELL COUNTY.

I arrived in Georgia, from Orleans county, Vermont, in September, 1851, and have lived in this county since 1852. I am a silversmith by trade, but have taught school several years.

There is not much inducement for silversmiths to come into this section. Money is scarce, and people very economical, rarely having work done unless compelled by necessity. There is not much demand or many openings for mechanics or trades-people.

Good hands on the farm can always get plenty of work at fair wages. The coldest weather I ever saw in Georgia, the thermometer was 6° above zero. The soil here is ... ...r than in Vermont, and can be improved at less trouble and expense. The productions are quite varied—those natural to a colder climate not as good as where it is colder, and those of a hotter climate requiring some protection in winter.

I consider this the most healthy section I ever lived in. Society is good and improving. A prudent man's life is as safe as anywhere in the world, and property is equally so from what I hear. Taxes are not exhorbitant. Immigrants are estimated by the stand they take in society, and by their general deportment. With the same industry and frugality, a man can make about twice as much as in Vermont.

CARROLL COUNTY.

My native State is Indiana. Settled in Georgia in 1872, and engaged in the business of traveling for a sewing machine company, which I have found profitable.

The climate is mild and delightful— can travel all through the winter with ease and comfort. The soil is moderately productive, but susceptible of a high degree of improvement ; produces in abundance corn, wheat, oats, Irish and sweet potatoes, grass, clover, fruit of all kinds and garden vegetables, (which can be grown the year round), and is well adapted to cotton. Health remarkable, the even temperature, abundance of clear, pure spring water, entire freedom from chills or epidemics, make this a desirable section for invalids. Society is good—a very large proportion of the people being members of the various religions denominations, and quiet, orderly, peaceable citizens. As to safety to life, I have traveled extensively in Georgia for the last seven years, all hours of day and night ; never carried a pistol or other weapon, and never needed one. Have never been molested or insulted.   B. F. COTTON,
Carrollton, Ga.

CLARKE COUNTY.

My native country, Ohio; settled in Georgia in 1878 ; my business, merchant ; no inducements for merchants. Climate is healthier than Ohio. Soil not as well adapted to grain as Ohio ; better for cotton. Productions are not as good as Ohio, outside of cotton. Health is better here than Ohio. Condition of society is as good as at any place I ever have been. I feel safer here, as to life, than in Ohio, and as to property I feel equally safe. Taxes are lower by one-third than in Ohio. The feeling toward immigrants is very cordial, and they are welcome. The price of land is very low compared to other States. The average price of land here is $8 per acre for good land. Labor very cheap (colored labor).   LUE MILLER, Athens, Ga.

CLAYTON COUNTY.

Ireland is my native land. I settled in Georgia in 1869, and engaged in farming and gardening, which I find pays a working man handsomely. The climate is healthy as any I ever lived in—in fact, I would not exchange with any State in the Union on this point.

Some soil is fertile, and some is pretty poor. I raise almost every known variety of vegetables successfully. With few exceptions, society is good. The laws are good, and those concerning protection to life and property are, in general, faithfully executed. The feeling towards immigrants is good. If they are honorable and industrious, they are well received—the same as natives. Land is very cheap compared to some other States, especially when we consider the great conveniences of good railroads, good markets, good water and good health. Some lands are as fine as I ever saw anywhere.
W. H. HARRISON, Hapeville, Ga.

COLUMBIA COUNTY.

We came with our family from Michigan nearly ten years ago, and commenced farming. We soon became acquainted with our neighbors, associating with them as we did with our Northern friends, expressing our opinions with the same freedom as in the North, and have never had any reason to complain of any ill treatment from Southerners.
W. H. COLLINS, Harlem, Ga.

I came from New York State to this State and county in 1865. Have been engaged in farming and manufacturing. If there is any ill-feeling against Northern settlers I have failed to discover it. I have never had a desire to return to New York; I like this climate and people better.   H. A. COOK, Harlem, Ga.

COWETA COUNTY.

I am not yet a citizen of the State, having come here from the North for the purpose of seeing, and getting all the information I can.

I can state, from my own experience, that the people of the South are the contrary of those in the North in several respects. They are the most benevolent and hospitable people, especially towards immigrants. The climate of North Georgia, I think, is the best in the world; the soil is good, and, with little pains, can be made rich. The products of the soil are small grain, corn, cotton, and especially all kinds of vegetables and fruits. Everything finds a ready market, and the most astonishing thing to me is, that the price of grain is the same as in my native country, Germany, where lands are worth from $300 to $600 per acre, while good lands can be bought here for $10, which will produce, on an average, very near the same. The taxes here are so little that they are not worth talking about. I have been here nearly a year, and will make this my permanent home after settling my business in Europe.   OTTO OTTENS, Newnan, Ga.

I am from Vermont, and came to Coweta county in 1844. My profession has been and is that of a teacher. As to inducements presented to those of my own profession, I will simply remark, "There is always room on the top shelf." As to climate—All things considered, there is no better outside of heaven. The soil is good enough for any one that will work, producing everything essential to comfort and prosperity. There is no healthier country on earth, in my opinion; the society is refined and elevated; and security of life and property unsurpassed anywhere. Taxes are very light. The feeling towards and treatment of immigrants is the same as towards natives of the same grade. Lands CHEAP, when the location, climate, society and natural advantages of this county are considered.   M. P. KELLOGG, Newnan, Ga.

DOUGLAS COUNTY.

I am a Canadian by birth, but was reared in the States of New York and Ohio. I was living in Ohio when the war broke out; served in the Federal army the whole war; was mustered out at Atlanta in January, 1866; never went back North, but remained in and about Atlanta; have resided in the counties of Fulton and Cobb, and now live in Douglas; am an architect and builder by profession. I planned and supervised the building of Governor Bullock's famous $20,000 barn. I have traveled the United States from Maine to Michigan, from Canada to Florida, and can say with truth, that where I have been in Georgia, and especially where I now live, is as healthy as any part of the world; and the climate is the most agreeable in this county of any place I ever saw. The soil is gray, yielding well with good cultivation. It is more profitable to raise corn here than in Ohio, because it can be sold at our own door at the same price as Ohio corn after being shipped here. Land from $1.00 to $15.00 per acre, according to condition and improvements. Anything that will grow in New York or Ohio will grow equally well here. Life and property are as safe here as anywhere in the Union. Immigrants will meet with a welcome. There is no social or political ostracism. Every man in this town knew that I served and was an officer in the Union army; yet last January they elected me town Recorder, giving me a majority of three to one over one of our merchants doing business here. Does that look like sectional hatred of Northern men? There is none of it here.   A. L. GOSLINE, Douglasville, Ga.

I emigrated from Iowa to Douglas county in 1869, and engaged in farming. Any man of energy can do well farming here, and a good mechanic can always get employment at from $1 to $3 a day. The climate is mild and pleasant, and the soil produces cotton, wheat, oats, rye, etc., very well. In fact, we can raise anything here that can be raised in any country, and everything we make finds a ready market at good prices. I have been in eleven different States, and have never seen a more healthy country than this, nor a more civil and law-abiding community. Immigrants from the North, or anywhere, are treated with the greatest civility and kindness, and life and property are safe as anywhere. I have been treated as well as a Southern man could be.

TIMOTHY RIDLEN, Wilsonville, Ga.

FAYETTE COUNTY.

I immigrated to this country from Germany in 1857, and have been farming for the last fourteen years. The climate is very pleasant and agreeable; the soil red and sandy, producing abundantly corn, wheat, oats, barley, rye, Irish and sweet potatoes and cotton. It is as healthy as any country on the globe, and the condition of society is all that could be desired. When a man is peaceable and well behaved himself, there is no danger to his life; and everybody, white and black, is made to abide the law. The very best of feeling prevails toward immigrants. Everybody is anxious for a better class of laboring people.

ABRAHAM STEINHEIMER.
Brooks' Station, Ga.

FULTON COUNTY.

I came here last July from the West, purchased a farm near this city, on which I now reside. As far as health is concerned, I affirm from my own experience and observation that there is no section where the climate, etc., is more conducive to this great blessing.

I have received none other than the kindest treatment from people of all social conditions. I find the upper classes social, obliging and courteous. I have had no reason to regret my coming to Georgia. The climate, so far as my brief experience, extends, is mild, agreeable and congenial. I find no difficulty in working out doors, summer and winter, when the weather is not stormy. None of my family has experienced any ill effects from the change of climate.

The soil is neither bad nor good, but is moderately fair agricultural soil—far better, however, than I anticipated—which will, by good culture and moderate fertilizing, give fair crops, from which more money can be realized, with less labor, than in many parts of the West.

I have seen no reason to regard any man's life unsafe who is not a rowdy or a courter of broils. I have no dread in this regard. More money can be made out of these lands by farming, gardening and stock-raising, than in most parts of the West.

My conversations with other Northern people I find residing here, lead me to believe that every man who comes to Georgia with a little capital, and who behaves himself as becomes a man, can and will do much better than in a new country. I came here with some severe prejudices against Southern people, but am now frank to confess that they have not been confirmed. I have no desire to leave this country, but feel contented and satisfied, and believe that all good citizens who come South will be as cordially received and as kindly treated by the Southern people as I have been.

I. ADOLPHUS, M.D., Atlanta, Ga.

Saxony (Germany) is my native country, from which I emigrated in 1842, and settled in Wisconsin, where I lived for 23 years. I came to Georgia in 1865, and engaged in raising farm and garden products. The inducements in all professions are innumerable to all who are willing to labor. There is no place or city in the United States where business of every kind is more lively, and honest labor more justly rewarded. The climate is a perfect representation of Italy—the finest in the world. The soil, properly managed, is most productive. The productions are a combination of both Northern and Southern States; for Georgia, in climate and soil, has the advantages of both sections. The people are most hospitable and kind to immigrants ; the motto " Welcome " might be appropriately inscribed on every door.

FRED. DECKNER, Atlanta, Ga.

After a long delay, I fulfill my promise to inform you how long I have been in this country, and how I am pleased with it. So long as I have been here, the most of the time I have been in the South, and it pleases me very well. I have earned much money, more than I ever could in Germany, for the Americans pay better than the Germans. Eighteen years I have been in the country, and always healthy. I have seen good times and bad, but it suits me very well, if only the German freedom and unity were here. You must excuse me that I write so badly, since I have not had a pen in my hand in eighteen years.

CHRISTIAN RUNGE, Hapeville, Ga.

GREENE COUNTY.

I am a farmer and a native of New York State. Came to Georgia in 1870. The inducements for farmers presented by this county are : Good land—land which responds most readily to good treatment; a climate such that the farmer can plow and sow or plant during all the months in the year ; great abundance of the best of water, from springs and wells ; good and cheap labor ; favorable conditions for the breeding of cattle sheep and horses ; good timber, etc. The climate is delightful as compared with that of New York or other Northern States. The winters are mild, with seldom frost enough to make a crust on the ground. The summers are warm, but pleasant.

The soil was originally good, much of it is thin from bad treatment, but is capable of improvement. The chief productions are cotton, all kinds of grain, vegetables and fruits common at the North, and a great many in addition. I believe this section (Middle Georgia) is as healthy as any in the world. Society is settled, and safety to life and property perfect, so far as I can judge, after nearly ten years experience and observation. Taxes are very light. The disposition towards immigrants is generally friendly. I have had no fault to find on this score The same amount of money in labor and land will give better results than in New York.

J. B. Y. WARNER,
Greensboro, Ga.

HANCOCK COUNTY.

I am by profession an architect, but have been farming since last year. I came from Massachusetts. I *think* that *farmers*—good and energetic *farmers*—can find no better State in the Union in which to settle, and I have lived in many States—North, South, East and West, including Texas and California—but as my experience in farming is very limited, my opinions are not entitled to much weight. A new country is not the home for an architect.

The climate is healthy, reaching neither extreme of heat or cold, and the white laborer is enabled to do field work winter and summer, and our stock. in general, can graze on prepared pasture or on swamp cane in winter.

I have met with such treatment as every man deserves who is a *man*, and all who cannot come under this head, in my humble opinion, had better stay away from Georgia, for they will here find *men* with whom to compete.

R. H. SALTER, Jr., Sparta, Ga.

I came from my native country—Canada—in 1865. I am a blacksmith by trade. The inducements for those of my trade are not very good. Many first-class mechanics have been compelled to go into other business.

The climate is the best I have ever experienced, and the soil good and very productive. Health good, and society as good as can be found. Life and property are as safe or safer than in any country. Industrious, well behaved immigrants are received kindly and well treated. Land ranges from $2 to $10 per acre, and the profits are good compared with other States and countries with which I am acquainted. I have lived in Canada and Michigan, and traveled through many of the Southern and Western States. I prefer Georgia to any country I know of. ROBERT WILSON, Sparta, Ga.

JASPER COUNTY.

I came from Connecticut in 1874. Am a clerk and ex-merchant. I could not wish a more salubrious climate. The soil is productive under proper treatment. The productions are cotton, corn, wheat, oats, barley, rye, clover, potatoes, peas, sugar cane, millet, beets, carrots, turnips, etc., and fruits of all kinds. Health is generally good, and society as good as can be found ; but a more thorough enforcement of laws is needed. Some of the best men in the county are in favor of *good* immigrants We want no more *Swedes* like those heretofore imported. In prices and profits of lands, this country compares favorably with any other. L. W. HUBBARD, Monticello, Ga.

MORGAN COUNTY.

We are farmers, and came from New York State in 1871. The inducements for farmers and *first-class* mechanics, with moderate means, are good. The climate is all that could be desired. The soil is a mixture of red clay and sand—badly worn, but easily brought to high state of cultivation, giving large returns for fertilizers and labor. The staple products are corn, cotton, wheat, oats, barley, hay, sweet and Irish potatoes, ground peas, etc., with a variety of fruits and vegetables too numerous to mention.

The climate is very healthy, and the society as good as can be found anywhere. The feeling towards immigrants is friendly, but the people are not as sociable with strangers as are the people out West, but as much so as in any old settled country.

J. M. & P. M. GRIGGS, Madison, Ga.

Native state—New Jersey. Came to Georgia in 1871 and engaged in farming. The climate is all that could be desired. The soil, originally fertile, is greatly impoverished, but is susceptible of a high degree of improvement. Healthy locality. Condition of society good. Life and property safe as in the North or West. Immigrants are treated very kindly and neighborly. Wool growing more profitable than in Wisconsin, where I resided fifteen years I came to Georgia for a milder climate and better health, and have not been disappointed. JOHN H. MORGAN, Madison, Ga.

I am from Eastern Pennsylvania. Settled here in 1867, and have been farming constantly since. For ten years have been Clerk of the Superior Court. To a live, industrious farmer, this part of Georgia offers many inducements—the mild climate, productive and easily cultivated soil, and varied productions, chief among them cotton, which always sells for cash at every railroad station. This section is remarkably healthy, being entirely exempt from malarial fevers and epidemics. The majority of our native population are intelligent, noble-hearted and refined. The races live together harmoniously, and in perfect security of life and property. Industrious and upright people are welcomed here regardless of their political or religious views. All taxes assessed for the year 1878 aggregated seven mills on the dollar. County well timbered and well watered by small streams and springs of excellent water.

E. REYSER, Madison, Ga.

[Letter also received from Mr. A. Van Houten, Madison, Ga., but space forbids publication.]

OCONEE COUNTY.

I came from Massachusetts in 1850, and have been farming most of the time. I also run a shoe factory. The inducements for farming or shoe business are better than in Massachusetts. The climate here is the best in the world. The soil is very productive of corn, cotton, wheat, oats, sweet and Irish potatoes, rye, barley—in fact, everything you may want to raise. Very healthy, society good, and, so far as safety to life and property is concerned, I feel perfectly safe; have never been molested. Feeling towards immigrants from any quarter is good. Lands are much cheaper in Georgia than in any State I know of. I consider farming here a good business. I have made clear in one year, farming with two hands, $1,400. Did not work in the farm myself.

W. A. WOODIS, Watkinsville, Ga.

OGLETHORPE COUNTY.

I am a native of Maine, having emigrated to Georgia in 1863, and have been employed as a machinist from 1863 to 1869, at which time I turned my attention to and have been employed ever since in farming in Oglethorpe county, Ga. At the present time little or no inducement is offered to mechanics to settle in this section. The climate is peculiarly mild and agreeable at all seasons of the year, and the water is of the purest character. While immigrants from the North will find here comparatively little frost or snow to impede farm work in winter, they will experience no debilitating heat in summer. Although the soil is thin and, in many parts, much worn, it may be restored by the use of fertilizers and made to become very productive.

Wheat and cotton and corn are the principal crops, but all the cereals can be raised and sold at remunerative prices. For excellence and abundance of timber this section is unsurpassed.

No section of the Southern States is healthier than Oglethorpe county, Ga., from the fact that there is nothing to produce malaria or other diseases. The society of this county is as good as any in Georgia, and is remarkable for its purity. Strangers are treated with the utmost kindness, and are invariably befriended. The prices of lands are much lower than those of the Northern States, and immigrants will find it to their interest to settle in this section of Georgia.   S. BAILEY, Maxeys, Ga.

PIKE COUNTY.

I was born in Bavaria, Germany. Have been working for express and railroad companies; have always found plenty of work at good wages. The climate is excellent; much of the soil is thin, but with proper management, very productive of corn, cotton, etc. My health has always been good; society first rate; no unusual danger to life and property. Treatment of foreigners generally good. There always have been some men in this country who have a hatred for foreigners, because the latter often prosper where natives would perish. I can't see why this is so, but it is according to my observation, I always avoid such characters. Lands are very cheap—fertile farms can be had for from $5.00 to $20.00 per acre. I consider this county one of the best in the State.

H. H. SWATTS, Barnesville, Ga.

PUTNAM COUNTY.

I settled in Georgia in 1876, having moved from New York, my native State. My health has been much improved by the change. The summer here is similar to that of Westchester county, New York, but of longer duration. The winter is much warmer than that of New York. The soil here is naturally very good, and yields according to the amount of fertilizers applied with skillful hands. Cotton, corn, oats, wheat and sugar cane are the principal crops, named in the order of their importance.

Safety to property is as well guaranteed here as elsewhere, with the exception of small thefts by negroes, such as rails from fences for fuel, and small matters. Horses, blankets, harness, whips, etc., are as safe here without locks as under lock and key in New York. Life is safe ordinarily, and would always be in the absence of drunkenness; but no one need fear molestation on account of politics. Hanging being the penalty for murder, is almost always omitted, as in many other States, and the offenders often go free because of the severe penalty.

Immigrants, who are farmers, will find society such as they leave elsewhere. Scholarly men find scholarly men in the South; but mechanics settling in country towns will sadly miss the society of men of their own calling. But business is always open here, that will make any economical mechanic, whether blacksmith, wheelwright or other, a good income.   BENJAMIN W. HUNT, Eatonton, Ga.

TROUP COUNTY.

I was raised in New York State ; lived in Illinois from 1832 to 1869, coming to Georgia in the latter year, where I have followed the business of milling and farming. I think the inducements for immigration not good for separate families, but good for colonies. The climate is very fine ; the soil badly used up ; productio s—almost everything with fertilizers ; fruit very good. Society good, and safety to life and property as well assured as in Illinois. Lands are worth from $1.00 to $8.00 , or acre ; profits from 5 to 15 per cent., when rented to freedmen, and have been getting lower for the last five years. Profits would be fair if colonies would settle and raise sheep, cattle and horses, and make, instead of buying on credit, all their corn and meat.

WILSON ALLEN, LaGrange, Ga.

WALTON COUNTY.

Being as far as I know the only permanent Northern settler in Walton county, I gladly respond to your circular. I am a native of New York State ; I settled here in 1870, and have been farming since then. The inducements for those with some means, say $1,000 or upwards, who wish to procure a good and pleasant home, are good. To such I say come to Walton county, Georgia, where the whites have a majority, and negro labor is plenty. Those who depend on their labor for support and have nothing more, I would not advise to come here.

The climate we think is as good as can be found. Soil, red clay subsoil with sandy surface. All kinds of grain do remarkably well. Cotton is our money crop. With suitable preparation of the land, the grasses do well. Health is good ; everybody is peaceable and attend to their own affairs. I consider my life and property safer than if in New York. Taxes, 8 mills. I never could expect to be treated with more kindness and courtesy than I have met with here. The price of land is from $5 to $12 per acre. As to profits, I think where 4 per cent. on the capital invested is realized in the Northern States, 10 per cent. on the same can be realized here.

J. T. VALLANCE, Rutledge, Ga.

SOUTHWEST GEORGIA.

This section embraces all that country lying between the Ocmulgee and Allapaha rivers in the east, and the Chattahoochee river in the west; the northern boundary being a line from Macon to Columbus, and the State of Florida its boundary in the south. It comprises the following counties:

Baker,	Decatur,	Macon,	Stewart,
Berrien,	Dooly,	Marion,	Sumter,
Brooks,	Dougherty,	Miller,	Taylor,
Calhoun,	Early,	Mitchell,	Terrell, .
Chattahoochee,	Houston,	Muscogee,	Thomas,
Clay,	Irwin,	Quitman,	Webster,
Colquitt,	Lee,	Randolph,	Wilcox,
Crawford,	Lowndes,	Schley,	Worth,

Like Southeast Georgia, the entire region is tertiary. It is more broken, or rolling, than Southeast Georgia, and, with the exception of marl, buhr and limestone, is, in a great measure, destitute of rocks. It has also a great proportion of clay lands and oak and hickory forest growth, although much the larger part of it is a light sandy soil, and was originally covered with yellow or long-leaf pine.

4

Th: clay lands are generally very rich, and their fertility lasting; the pine la ids produce freely, are easil/ worked, but are l s4 durable, thou. h, with reasonable fertilization, will .ast for many years. The dis ri t contains very littl waste land, or lands too poor or too swampy for cultivati~n, while the alluvial lands of the Chattanoochee and Fint rivers, and of many of t .e creeks, a e made thi secti n famous as the best cotton region of the State. Corn, oats, wheat, rye and sugar-cane grow well.

The depth of the subs il beneath the surface on clay lands is 6 to 10 inches; on sandy lands, from 12 inches to 3 feet. The preponderating forest growth is long-leaf, or yellow, pine, furnishing the best of lumber, large quantities of which are prep re l annually for export and domestic use. The supply would seem to be almost inexhaustible. Spirits of turpentine, rosin, pitch and tar— all the products of this tree—are made in considerable quantities, and the interest is on the increase. In the swamps nd river bottoms there are cypress, cotton-wood, poplar, ash, maple, beach, birch, red-bay, magno ia, sweet-gum and water-oak; while the growth of the clay belts is red and post o ks, black jack, hickory, walnut, black-gum, logwood and buckeye.

Cotton is the lead.ng market crop of this division, and, previous to the derangement of plantation labor by emancipation, its crop of the staple probably equalled the roduction of all the rest of the State. Corn and oats grow to great perfection, but none for export since the war; sugar cane is a successful crop throughout the section; tobacco, in considerable quantities, is grown in the southern counties.

The average yields, per acre, with good cultivation, are: cotton, 500 lbs. in seed; corn, 10 bushels; oats, 15 bu hels; syrup, 200 gallons; sweet potatoes, 150 bushels; ground peas, 50 bushels. On best lands, without manure, 1,500 to 2,000 lbs. cotton in seed, 50 to 75 bushels corn, 50 to 65 bushels oats, 400 gallons of syrup, and 400 bushels sweet potatoes, are often produced. It is reliably reported that a Berrien county farmer produced 800 bushels of sweet potatoes on one acre, under high cultivation. Over 900 gallons of syrup per acre has been made in Thomas county.

Cotton is planted early in April, picking commences in August; corn planted in February and March, matures in August; oats sowed usually in November, harvested last of May to last of June; sugar-cane planted February and March, cut October and November.

Average wages of good farm hands, $9 per month; of ordinary mechanics, $1.25 to $2 per day.

The fruits best adapted to this section are the peach, pear, melon grape (especially the scuppernong), fig, pomegranate, some varieties of apple, strawberry; in the southern tier of counties, the orange, lemon and banana are successfully grown. There is no country where all the vegetables grow to great r perfection when cultivated with ordinary skill. The tea plant and the olive have also been successfully grown in this and other Southern divisions of the State.

The climate varies but little from that of Southeast Georgia, the average mean temperature being, in summer, 85°; in winter 65°—extremities, 94° and 32°. Snow falls about once in 10 or 15 years, never sufficiently to completely cover the ground. The health of the hill country and pine lands is good the year round, but fevers, generally of a mild type, are common along the lines of rivers and swamps in late summer and early fall months.

The country is well watered, and good water powers are found where the streams break through the marl beds, with which many of the counties abound. Several railroads traverse the section, while the Ocmulgee, Flint and Chattahoocee rivers furnish transportation nearly the entire year.

The poorer, unimproved pine lands, well timbered, may be bought at 50 cents per acre; good at $1 to $2.50; best lands at from $4 to $10—all on a liberal credit.

The drinking water in the hill country is good, though not very cold; in the flat lands not so good, and generally impregnated with lime. The waters abound with fish, and the forests furnish game, large and small, in any quantity desired.

The large bodies of unimproved land, to be found in nearly every county of the district, furnish excellent pasturage the year round for cattle and sheep, and are free to all. Little or no feeding or sheltering is required, and beef and mutton are taken directly from the range to market.

LETTERS FROM ACTUAL SETTLERS.

CALHOUN COUNTY.

My profession is that of architect. and my native State, New York. I came to Georgia in 1867, induced by the firm belief that with such endless resources this must ultimately rank as the first of the Southern States. The climate is most excellent—no such sudden changes in the weather occurring here as elsewhere in the State, or other States. The soil is good—stiff, gray and loamy, with red clay subsoil. Productions—most everything that grows. As to health—some portions are sickly, others as healthy as anywhere. Society good. and life and property as safe as anywhere. The treatment of immigrants is exceedingly kind and courteous. The prices of lands are very moderate, and in some cases very low, and the profits very good, compared with lands elsewhere at high prices; and where high culture is practiced, the results compare favorably with any portions of the Southern or Middle States, and in some cases, with the Western States.   W. H. PARKINS, Morgan, Ga.

CLAY COUNTY.

I am a merchant, a native of Bavaria, Germany, whence I came to Georgia in 1860. This is a good country for farmers and good mechanics. The climate is healthy. the soil mixed clay and light sand bottoms, and productive of corn, cotton, sugar-cane, potatoes. The society is very good, and life and property well protected. Taxes moderate. Immigrants would meet with good treatment and a warm welcome. Land worth $2.50 to $5.00, according to quality and improvements. Schools good.

ISAAC LOEB, Fort Gaines, Ga.

DOUGHERTY COUNTY.

You ask for my experience as an immigrant. I must say that it has been very pleasant, both socially and politically ; and as for health, I could not have found a more favorable climate. I am a farmer, and I think as an agricultural State Georgia, and particularly the southern part of it, is more favored both in soil and climate than almost any other section of America. One great advantage to immigrants is that we have every facility in the way of cheap transportation, by rail and by water. The productions of the soil are almost unlimited in variety and amount. Still there is room for choice in selecting lands, and one should not be too hasty in settling. The best time to visit this country is from September to June, for then you see the state at its best and worst. Lands from $3.00 to $8.00 per acre. Taxes very low. Stock of all kinds are raised here, and it is a great fruit country. I came from Maine in 1869.

F. L. BRIDGE, Albany, Ga.

I immigrated from England to Georgia in 1878, and am engaged as a clerk. My family and I have suffered less from *heat* than in Massachusetts.

The soil is a sandy loam, capable of a high degree of improvement. Have had better health than in Massachusetts. Society is good, and I consider life and property as safe as in the Northern States. The feeling towards immigrants is all that could be desired. The white people gladly welcome settlers from the other States, and give them every assistance in their power. Too much praise cannot be awarded them. Land is very low—much below its actual value. One or two farms adjoining me are for sale at a price much less than the cost of improvement thereon. The profits in good seasons will almost pay for a farm. A much better opportunity is offered immigrants here than at the West.

THOS. KIRKE, Albany, Ga.

LOWNDES COUNTY.

New Jersey is my native State, whence I came to Georgia in 1869, and engaged in farming and lumbering. The climate is *healthy*, if the diet be suited to the latitude, as is proven by the fact that the people are able to live on corn bread, bacon, coffee and syrup. It is not so hot as the Middle States in summer. The natural soil is much better, but does not retain manure so well on account of evaporation in winter. It is easier to work, being free from stones. I have raised 16½ bushels of Irish potatoes on one-twentieth of an acre. The second crop yields well, if of an early variety, furnishing a supply during the year. Not good for fruit, except figs, grapes and pears.

Horned cattle can be raised at one-fifth the expense required in the Middle States, requiring but a very small amount of nutritious food in winter, when the grass is tough. Life and property are as safe as in any country of mixed races. Negroes here, as elsewhere, are given to pilfering. Whites are easily angered, but not revengeful. Settlers are treated with kindness, both in social and business circles. Lands worth $5.00 per acre here, would sell for $50.00 in New York, Pennsylvania, or New Jersey.

L. A. HAYNES, Valdosta, Ga.

MUSCOGEE COUNTY.

My native place is New York City. I settled in Georgia in 1824, and followed merchandising and farming in Florida and Georgia for thirty-three years ; and for the last twenty-eight years I have also been engaged in manufacturing in Columbus, Ga., and it is my principal business, though I have also a farm.

For manufacturing there is a wide field open. The advantages of cheap material, climate (and consequently moderately low wages), unused and abundant water power, cheap coal, home markets for goods, defy competition. And when home markets are supplied. Southern mills can still ship yarns or goods to the North, or any country cheaper than they can produce them. Farming can be, and is, made profitable, and affords a sure living.

The climate is not only healthful, but we are free from cholera, yellow fever, or other malignant disease. Whites and blacks work in the fields and shops all the day long and all the year round. Sunstrokes are unknown. The winters are mild. but ice often forms one-half inch or more thick. It is sufficiently cold to invigorate the system for the summer work.

Life and property are as secure as in any country in the world. Immigrants from any State of the Union. or any foreign country, are kindly received, and a helping hand is extended to all comers, if found worthy; and they will be received in any society to which they may be entitled by their intelligence and moral conduct. Society is good, public and private schools for all. and churches of all denominations. There is, strictly speaking. no *class* society. Integrity, honesty, industry and fair intelligence are the qualifications for good society. Without these, wealth alone has no influence. The masses of the people are fairly educated, and all are kind and social. This is no place for persons who would seek soft places or easy times without industry and application on their part.   W. H. YOUNG, Columbus, Ga.

RANDOLPH COUNTY.

Born in Ireland. My boyhood was spent in Franklin county, New York. Educated at the French college, Montreal, Canada. Came to Georgia in 1851. I have been a teacher ever since.

There is plenty of employment for good teachers. The climate is pleasant and healthy. The soil is productive. As a wheat-growing country, this is not surpassed by Northern New York. We raise Irish potatoes, cabbage, oats, rye, barley, etc., equal to New York. Georgia has as good and genial a climate as any country on earth. And a more congenial and social people lives no where on earth, except Canada and Virginia. It makes no difference where a man is from, he is here treated according to his merits, and no country offers finer inducements to immigrants. There is not one word of truth in all the slanderous and murderous reports from the South circulated through the North.

                          M. A. McNULTY, Cuthbert, Ga.

SCHLEY COUNTY.

I am a native of Edinburgh Scotland; have been living in the South ever since 1840. Came first to Montgomery. Ala., and lived in different parts of that State until 1857, when I moved my family to Sumter county, Ga. If I have any profession it is that of a seaman, but, since living in the South, have been a school teacher, a book-keeper and a scrivener. From my own experience I am free to say (and qualify to it if necessary), that there is *no* country (and I have been in many) where there are more or greater inducements to settle—strangers. emigrants of all grades, trades and professions—than in Alabama and Georgia. The climate is mild and pleasant; the soil, when fresh. exceed ingly productive. Small grain of all kinds—wheat and oats especially—are easily and abundantly produced. So with corn, peas, potatoes and other esculent roots. Vegetables of every kind may be successfully cultivated, and the want of a good garden in any family may be truthfully attributed to carelessness, if not to laziness Fruits of many varieties—nearly all European, and some tropical fruits—are grown profusely. Peaches, apples, pears, plums, strawberries, etc., grow as if indigenous to the country. I have not seen many wild fruits, but blackberries (known in Scotland as the brambleberry) and the huckleberry (in Scotland the blueberry) are plentiful and free to a l—*the orchard of the poor*. I have been very healthy since living in the South; have raised a family of five children, and during thirty-eight years all the sickness will not amount to more than four or five months, all put together; and where I have lived I have not seen a great deal of sickness, though I believe my family is an exception, there having been better health among them generally than among my neighbors. The moral condition of society is generally good, and will compare favorably with that of any other country.

Life is as safe and property as secure as in any other country, and much more so than in many which I have visited. *Until the close of the late war*, there were but few locks in the neighborhood where I lived; since then, however, we have had greater use for them.

The amount of taxes depends entirely on the financial condition of the State and the county in which a person lives. I have always found the taxes lighter than in my native country. The feeling manifested to strangers is always kind; a sober, well-behaved person is invariably well received and hospitably entertained; and if his manners and conduct be that of a gentleman, he is at once put on an easy footing and soon made to feel at home The *social* treatment of any person in the South depends on himself. If his conduct be good and his deportment civil and obliging, he will be treated kindly and courteously, and more like a friend than a mere acquaintance. If an emigrant, he will not only be treated kindly, etc., but he will be assisted in every reasonable way. After an experience of nearly forty years among the people of the South, I can truly say that they are the most hospitable, generous and charitable people that I have ever met with in *all my travels*. "Gentility" seems to be instinctive with the majority. No emigrant, whether capitalist or laborer, need fear to come South on the ground of uncivil treatment or unfriendly reception; for either will be warmly welcomed, and capital and labor can find no better investment or safer depository—the stories of Southern outrage to the contrary notwithstanding, and (" not to put too fine a point upon it ") they, in nine cases out of ten, are simply "gratuitous.'

W. C. P. CLEGHORN, Ellaville, Ga.

TAYLOR COUNTY.

Logan county, Kentucky, is my native place. I came to Georgia in 1865 as a farmer. The inducements to farmers are good. The climate is pleasant and healthful; society good, and life and property as safe as could be desired. The treatment of immigrants is most kind and hearty. Lands low and profits good. This is one of the best countries for laboring men I have ever seen. All supplies, except coffee, can be successfully produced here. Provisions and other supplies plentiful and cheap.

W. C. EDMONDSON, Butler, Ga.

TERRELL COUNTY.

Born in Salisbury, Connecticut; settled in Georgia in 1869; steam saw mill and lumber business. Inducements equal to any State as far as my knowledge goes or extends for mine or other professions. Climate the best I ever lived in. Soil, axcellent; productions not to be equalled in proportion to cultivation. Health—no need to ever get ick, only by imprudence. Society good; life and property perfectly safe; taxes about right; a general desire for immigration; prices and profits of lands about equal to other adjoining States.

WILLIAM A. PEET, Dawson, Ga.

THOMAS COUNTY.

My original profession was that of a confectioner, but for the last ten years I have been engaged in growing fruits, having come to this State in 1850. There is but little inducement for mechanics to settle here, because everything that can be made abroad is brought here for sale.

The climate is all that could be desired. The soil is of varied character, light soils predominating, but all produce well with a moderate use of manures. The productions include about all those of the temperate and semi-tropical zones. The health and physical development of the people are specially good, and I find that foreigners here enjoy permanent good health. This is the general rule with all those who retain their old habits of using lighter food and drink than are here commonly used. The condition of society here is very good. The foreign immigran would perhaps miss the jovial festivals he had so often enjoyed in his old home.

Ten years ago, when I brought here two Swiss families, the head of one, shortly after their arrival, exclaimed : " My God ! can you let your hogs run about as they do, without their being stolen ?" Even my tempting fruits are not trespassed upon by the boys here in town.

Taxes are very light compared to elsewhere. Very kind feelings are manifested towards the immigrant who settles here as a worker, and not as an agitator. His standing in society will be equal to his reasonable expectations, here or elsewhere.

JOHN STARK, Thomasville, Ga.

I am a native of the United States (North) ; settled in Thomasville in 1873. Am a minister of the Gospel. The inducements for immigration are reasonably good. The climate is delightful ; the soil, though not naturally rich, is easy of improvement. Productions, cotton, corn, oats, wheat, rye, rice, flax, broom-corn, sugar-cane, sweet and Irish potatoes, strawberries, pears, peaches, grapes, etc. General healthfulness excellent. Condition of society and safety to life and property good. There is a great desire for immigrants, and they are kindly treated. Lands are low in price, and profits of farming remunerative. Wise investments in farming lands, with suitable management, yields a handsome profit, despite the expensive transportation, which in *some* cases is ruinous, and in all a serious drawback.

JAMES A. McREE,
Thomasville, Ga.

[A letter containing substantially the same representations as the foregoing, was received from Mr. Fay Hirshinger, a native of Germany, now merchandising in Thomasville.]

WORTH COUNTY.

My native country is England, whence I came in 1856 to Irwin county. Have followed school teaching and planting. Men with small capital can do more and better here than anywhere I know of. Good teachers make a living. Climate is good, soil various, but all will remunerate labor properly directed. Productions are corn, cotton, potatoes, etc., etc. Fruits and vegetables in abundance. Health good, society coarse, but honest. Life and property are safe. Taxes light Treatment of strangers is very kind and hospitable. · Land is cheaper in this section, according to quality, than anywhere else.

E. COURTOY, Isabella, Ga.

I came from Ohio to Georgia in the month of December, 1872, and have been engaged in farming ever since. I made two crops in Fulton county, and one in Fayette county. From thence I moved to Worth county, where I have purchased a lot of land and established a permanent home, having my second crop about ready to "lay by." I am satisfied that I can make farming profitable here, simply by leaving off guano and manufacturing my own manure. The climate surpasses that of any other country I ever saw. The winters are mild, and I have suffered much less from heat in the summer season than in Ohio The soil, in places, is sandy, while other places are pebbly and solid, and produces well by using but a trifle of manure. The production of this country is about the same as that of Ohio, with the addition of much that cannot be raised in that State. This country is very healthy, except malarial diseases about the water-courses; society is about the same as in Ohio; so is the security of life and property. Taxes are no higher here than in any other country. The feeling and treatment manifested towards me, wherever I have lived in this State, have been nothing but friendship and kindness. Lands here rate from 50 cents to $3 00 per acre. Thousands of acres of unimproved lands in this county can be bought at 50 cents per acre, much better and more profitable to farmers than lands in Ohio and elsewhere for which you have to pay from $40.00 to $50.00 per acre.

JOHN MYGRANT, Warwick, Ga.

EAST GEORGIA.

This section of the State embraces the country lying between the heads of tide water in the east, and the Ocmulgee river in the west, and south to the corner of Liberty, Tatnall and Appling, and embraces the following counties:

Bull ch,	Jefferson,	Pulaski,	Telfair,
Burke,	Johnson,	Richmond,	Twiggs,
Dodge,	Laurens,	Screven,	Washington,
Emanuel,	Montgomery,	Tatnall,	Wilkinson.
Glasscock,			

It differs from Middle Georgia in several important respects: its geological formations are tertiary instead of metamorphic; its average elevation is only about 250 feet above the sea; its surface is more level; its soils, for the most part, loamy or sandy; subsoil clay, red and yellow, four to six inches below the surface in clay lands, ei ht to twelve inches in sandy lands; its forest growth is principally pine; it contains calcareous marls in considerable deposits. It is also the commencement of the section in which the sugar cane can be profitably cultivated, while its rocks, which are few, are of a sedimentary character, with iron ore and Buhr stone in several localities. D posits of kaolin and pipe clay are found along its entire length from east to west. Its water powers are less than those of Middle Georgia, and its drinking wat r, while good, is less cool and pure. While pine is the leading forest growth and the chief timber for building and export, there are also large bodies of oak and hickory. The soils in such localities ar either clayey or gray, mostly the latter, and admirably adapted to the production of cotton and corn; cypress abounds in the swamps and lowlands. The county of Burke was, for many years, and until the late revolution in our system of labor, the leading cotton producing county of the State. The comparatively fresh lands of Decatur have, of late years, enabled her to claim and hold the championship in this particular product. Cotton, with corn, wheat (the adaptation to which lessens as we proceed southward into the pine lands), oats, rye, barley, sugar cane, potatoes, constitute the staple products of the section. The average yields per acre, with fair culture, are, cotton, 650 lbs.; corn, 14 bushels; wheat, 12 bushels; oats, 25 bus els; cane syrup, 300 gallons; potatoes, 150 bushels; barley, 30 bushels. There is much high culture in the district, and these results are often quadrupled. The seasons for planting and harvesting are near the same.

EMANUEL COUNTY.

I came to Georgia from New Hampshire in 1854 left it in 1859 and returned in 1869 and have since been engaged in the lumber business, as proprietor of saw mills in Emanuel county and in Savannah. I consider Emanuel county as healthy as New Hampshire.

The soil, though thin, produces well when fertilized and properly worked. As to the condition of society and the safety to life and property, it is equal to any section of the country. During my residence of six years in the county, I did not keep a yard dog, and in warm weather doors and windows were left open at night without fear of intruders.

From my own experience, I can commend the State of Georgia and its people to all who desire to change their residence, assuring them that (in my opinion) no State offers greater inducements to the right kind of men. With land at 50c. to $2.50 per acre, State and county tax 8 mills on the dollar, a good climate, every one ought to succeed. There are rare chances here for energetic men with small capital—chances not all taken up as in the North. I have lived in New York, New Hampshire, Massachusetts, Michigan, Illinois, Indiana, South Carolina, Louisiana and Mississippi, but all things considered, I prefer to live in Georgia.   HORACE P. SMART, Savannah, Ga.

I am by trade a machinist, and came to this country from England in 1849. Have been in the saw mill business since 1851. Inducements are not as good as when I first came here. I am well pleased with the climate. The soil is not very good, but with manure produces well. corn, cotton, potatoes and sugar cane. Health has been good. Strangers are well treated if well behaved. Land from 50 cents to $1.00 per acre.
                   GEORGE GARBUTT, 9½ C. R. R., Ga.

PULASKI COUNTY.

I immigrated from Massachusetts, my native State, to Georgia in 1877, and have been engaged in the mercantile business and in farming, almost exclusively the latter last year. Although the methods of farming here are different from what I have been accustomed to, yet such information was readily obtained as enabled me to make with three plows, 24 bales of cotton, 700 to 800 bushels of corn, and a good crop of peas. Labor—the main factor here—requires more study than any of the elements of successful farming. My observation, thus far, teaches me that by personal attention to business, by patience and strict justice and fair dealing towards employees, the mutual interests of both white and colored people may be promoted and prosperity secured.

For three months of the year—July, August and September—the weather is very warm, though the thermometer seldom rises above 90 or 95 degrees in the shade. During the remaining months the climate is delightful. Although not much of the soil is naturally rich, yet it is easily worked, and by intelligent cultivation, produces profitable crops. It is mostly sandy upon a subsoil of stiff clay. The forest growth is chiefly pine and oak, though there are many other species. The staple products are cotton, corn, oats, sugar cane and sweet potatoes, with a great variety of garden vegetables. Peaches, sand pears, grapes, plums, strawberries, etc., can be raised in abundance. One party here made 1,200 gallons of wine from three acres of Concord and Delaware grapes—the fourth season after setting.

Any industrious, sober man, with a small capital, by accommodating himself to the methods of farming suited to this region (a matter not at all difficult), is almost sure to "get on" here; and in a few years, if he proves himself trustworthy, can work himself up to actual ownership and independence.   . B. F. PURSONS,
                                                 Hawkinsville, Ga.

RICHMOND COUNTY.

I am from Brooklyn, New York, and settled in this county in 1870. Before coming South I was in the mercantile business, but have since been farming successfully. I find the climate all that could be desired, as we do not have in summer the sultry atmosphere of New York, while the winters are just cool enough to invigorate the system without causing inconvenience. The soil is not naturally very rich, but susceptible of high cultivation by use of manures. The river bottoms are as rich as land ever gets to be. We grow cotton, corn, melons, sweet potatoes, wheat, oats and hay for market; while the kitchen garden affords *all* the vegetables that grow in any climate. It is rarely that we hear of sickness in the neighborhood, and society is refined and cultivated. Life and property, in my mind, are safer here than in the city of New York. Taxes are very light indeed. Every encouragement is offered to persons who come here in good faith, with a view to actual settlement; and all such will meet with great cordiality and good will. With the exception of *apples*, we grow all kinds of fruit to perfection.

FRED. LITTLE, Allen's Station, Ga.

SCREVEN COUNTY.

I am a Prussian, and landed in New York in 1867. In 1868 I concluded to move to Florida, but did not get further than Charleston, as the connecting steamer left before we got in. Not liking the idea of stopping in a hotel for a week, with a large family, I determined to settle in Georgia, took the train for Augusta at once, and found employment in a carpenter shop. I am an architect and carpenter by trade, and earned a good support for a mother, a wife, and seven small children (the eldest nine years)

Not liking town life, in 1869 I moved to Screven county, rented a small tract of land, and run a one-horse farm. The place proved sickly, being very near to the river swamp, and the next year I moved four miles off, on the high land, first rented and then bought a cotton plantation. The climate is delightful—a little warm in summer, but the winter just about cold enough to keep a man healthy. Except a bone-felon, I have never had any sickness in my family, and the people here die mostly from *old age* or accident.

The soil is generally light, but with a good home-made fertilizer, almost anything can be raised. I planted last year, for trial, one acre in oats, well manured with cotton seed and lime, and threshed seventy-five bushels. We can raise with success cotton, oats, rye, corn, rice, peas, sugar cane, Irish and sweet potatoes and melons. Wheat is liable to rust. Of vegetables, almost anything will succeed that is planted, and with very little trouble we can have them fresh the year round, and never have to store them.

Society is very good, and an industrious immigrant, if he can show an honest face and has a good will to work, will find an open door and a hearty welcome everywhere. My house door I never lock at night, and I have never carried a weapon for self-defense. I live right in the heart of the so-called Ku-Klux, but never have seen or heard anything of it, except in *Northern papers*.

The price of farms range from $3.00 to $10.00 per acre, and several owners of large tracts of land will give favorable terms to immigrants. If a man has a horse and money to buy one year's provisions to start with, he can't help from improving every year. If I can be of any service to such persons as may wish to settle here, I will take it as a favor to hear from them.   A. BEWAN, Mobley's Pond, Ga.

WASHINGTON COUNTY.

Came from Delaware, fall of 1877. Business—gas and steam fitting. No inducements for others in this branch. The climate is temperate and agreeable—more so than I expected. Soil thin, loamy—very easily cultivated, and capable of producing very good crops by a slight addition of fertilizers. Main productions—cotton and corn. Good fruit country. Tolerably good for grain; can raise, on an average, more and better oats than in the North. In fact, anything that can be raised anywhere (excepting the tropics) can be successfully grown here. My health was never better, and I consider the country very healthy indeed. Society is very good; the people generally very sociable. My being a *yankee* has not made one jot of difference in my social relations; in fact, I think it has given, or tended to give, a sort of popularity, the same that I have sometimes seen experienced by Southerners in the North. I am running a steam mill and cotton gin—a business that brings me face to face with most every one in this section, and I am not aware that I have ever been the object of ill feeling. Life and property extremely safe. Immigrants who come here are welcomed and assisted. The *best lands* can be had for $10.00 per acre.

HENRY T. HAYES, Tennille, Ga.

[Reference is made to Mr. Carl J. Mort, a Swede, who came to Georgia in 1850. Postoffice, Sandersville, Georgia.]

WILKINSON COUNTY.

Born in Germany. Settled in Georgia in 1870, as a hotel keeper and farmer. Inducements to immigrants only moderate. Climate unsurpassed. On flat lands the soil is light and sandy; on the rolling lands, it is a good loam, with clay subsoil. Healthy in elevated portions, but in summer and fall the flat and river lands somewhat sickly. Condition of society is good, including schools and churches. Life and property amply protected by law. Feeling towards immigrants good, and they will be well received. Prices of good cleared lands are reasonable. Wild lands very cheap. Profits are limited, compared with the Western country, on account of old worn lands and difficulty of controlling labor.   O. H. L. STRUBING, Toomsboro, Ga.

My native country is Cavan county, Ireland. I settled in Georgia in 1851, and engaged in farming. All who work can live well. The climate is mild and healthy, and the soil productive of a great variety of crops, comprising everything usually grown in the temperate zone, especially corn, cotton, wheat, oats, potatoes, peas, melons, and all kinds of fruit. The health is as good as anywhere in Georgia, and society first-class. Life and property are as safe as anywhere on the face of the earth. Taxes are low. The feeling towards immigrants the kindest in the world to all who deserve. Land ranges from $3.00 to $7.00 per acre. Profits are good, according to industry, and costs of hiring as low as anywhere. Religion is free to all. All persons can worship according to their own consciences. The right to vote is freely accorded to all, each and every one voting as he pleases.   PATRICK DONALLY, Gordon, Ga.

SOUTHEAST GEORGIA.

This section comprises the coast and tide-water section of the State, and embraces fifteen counties, as follows:

Appling,	Chatham,	Effingham,	Pierce,
Bryan,	Clinch,	Glynn,	Ware,
Camden,	Coffee,	Liberty,	Wayne.
Charlton,	Echols,	McIntosh,	

The entire region is tertiary, and mostly without rocks. It is the last formed and first settled portion of Georgia, and its area of dry land is being gradually added to year after year through the action of the tides. It is low and level, the average elevation being less than 100 feet.

It has three distinct soils: 1. Light, sandy and poor; 2. Dark sandy loam, containing a large amount of vegetable matter; 3. Reddish and clayey. The first is naturally unproductive, and covered with stunted pines and saw palmetto, but swamp muck being abundant, with a proper distribution of it over the land, it may be cultivated with reasonable success. The second variety is covered with a natural growth of yellow pine, magnolia, red bay, live-oak, cedar and cabbage palmetto, and in productiveness is excelled by no land in the State; it has a yellow clay subsoil, varying from ten inches to three feet; sea-island cotton, corn and sugar-cane grow in the greatest luxuriance. The third variety is also very productive, pine, oak, hickory and gum being the prevailing forest growth; subsoil clay, red and yellow; average depth below the surface, eight to twelve inches. It is the great rice-producing section of the State—the broad bottoms of the Savannah, the two Ogeechees, the Altamaha and Saltilla being devoted almost exclusively to that cereal. It is also grown to a less extent on the St. Mary's, and considerable quantities on inland swamps, the irrigation in the latter bieng effected by means of "backwater" collected from rains and secured by dams. Sea-island, or long staple cotton, was the only variety formerly grown, but of late years the short staple has been introduced and cultivated with fair success. Corn, oats, pumpkins, potatoes, ground-peas, all do well· The sea-islands are devoted almost exclsively to cotton, corn, cane, fruits and vegetables. Cypress and palmetto abound in the swamps and river bottoms.

Average yield, per acre, of staple crops, with fair cultivation : Sea-island cotton, 600 lbs. in seed ; corn, 15 bushels ; oats, 25 bushels ; rice, 40 bushels ; cane syrup, 300 gallons, potatoes, 200 bushels. On best lands, 1,500 lbs. seed cotton, 60 bushels rice, 600 gallons syrup, 50 bushels corn, 40 bushels oats, 400 bushels potatoes are often produced on one acre. Corn planted middle of February till 1st of June, gathered in August and September ; cotton planted in March and April, gathered in autumn months ; rice planted March to June, harvested last of August till 1st October ; cane planted February and March, cut in October and early in November ; potatoes planted March to June, gathered July to November ; oats sowed in October, harvested in May.

Average wages of good farm hands per month, with rations, $9 ; of ordinary mechanics, $1.50 to $2.50 per day.

The fruits best adapted to the soil and climate, are the figs, melons of all kinds, scuppernong grapes, pomegranates, sand or LeConte pears, some varieties of apples, strawberries ; the orange, lemon, lime and banana are also grown successfully.

This section exports annually large quantities of fruits, chiefly melons—also vegetables ; nearly every variety of the latter attains to great perfection.

The climate is delightful in winter, the mean temperature being about 48° ; nor is the heat oppressive in summer, 79° being the mean temperature. The mercury seldom rises above 90° or falls below 32°. The bracing influences of the sea-breezes is felt throughout this section. Snow is rarely seen, and never sufficient to lie on the groud half a day. Along the coast and off the fresh water rivers, the section is among the healthiest in the State.

The district is well watered by running streams, and all parts of it convenient to market. Drinking water, though not cold, is good and wholesome. Railroads penetrate every county, except two, and they are well supplied with navigable streams, connecting with inland steamboat navigation from Savannah to Florida. The pine lands of this section are well timbered, and under good culture, produce fine crops. It may be bought at from 50 cents to $2.00 per acre, and on a liberal credit; improved lands of the second quality mentioned, are worth from $5 to $10 per acre; good river rice lands, from $25 to $30 per acre.

In Effingham, Camden, Wayne and Charlton, there are large deposits of calcareous marl, where it can be utilized to the greatest advantage in agriculture. Our State Geologist, in commenting on this division of the State, uses the following language:

"I have seen no section of Georgia in which the people seem to secure a comfortable supply of food with less effort, and can see no reason why the whole country may not be made equal, if not superior, to that section of Prussia where Frederick the Great founded the city of Berlin, from which capital, within this decade, terms have been dictated to the continent of Europe. There is the greatest similarity in the soil and topography of the two sections, and, should the tide of German emigration be turned hither, there would soon be realized to them the comforts and pleasures of the Fatherland."

LETTERS FROM ACTUAL SETTLERS.

BRYAN COUNTY.

I came to this county from the North in 1850. The climate here is delightful, and the soil unsurpassed for rice, corn, peas, cotton, potatoes. As to health, there is some fever on the river, but very healthy away from it.

The condition of society is good, and there are very few disorderly persons in the part of the county where I live. Taxes are moderate, and life and property are as secure as anywhere in the Union. I think good immigrants would be very favorably received. The profits of rice culture are large, except when the crop is injured by storms, which are liable to occur in the river bottoms.

GEO. LYMAN, Appleton, 1¼ A. & G. R. R., Ga.

I am a native of Massachusetts—lived three years in New York State and two in Connecticut—settled in Bryan county, Ga., in 1867. I am a teacher and farmer. If money is the object, school teaching is not a success—though we need teachers—but farming pays. Timber—cypress, black gum, sweet gum, and especially pine—is abundant, and might be utilized in the manufacture of boxes and measures. The climate is delightful, and I think I owe my life to it, for I came here a consumptive and am cured without medicine. The pine land is light and poor, but yields ample returns when fertilizers are applied. A great deal of swamp land, not yet under cultivation, is very rich, and will be reclaimed in time. The leading farm crops are cotton, rice, sweet potatoes, sugar cane, corn, oats, peas, chufas. Have been married twelve years, have six children, none of us have been sick a day, had no occasion to call a doctor. The people are moral and generally religious; very few atheists, deists and sceptics. A fine opening for preachers and teachers who don't want much money for their services. I believe that life and property are as safe here as anywhere. The people are law-abiding. Taxes very low—only one per cent. including State and county. The feeling is very kind towards immigrants; the people are more anxious for immigration than the older States. Land will average about $1.00 per acre, and is capable of a high degree of improvement by proper use of fertilizers, at a much less cost than the soil in New York, Massachusetts or Connecticut.

CAMDEN COUNTY.

I am a native of New York State—did mercantile business for twenty years at Waverly, Tioga county, in that State ; came to Georgia for my health in 1869. Since my residence here—nearly ten years—myself and family have enjoyed uninterrupted health, winter and summer. From my experience and observation, I believe the climate of the Southern coast of Georgia cannot be surpassed for health and comfort during the entire year.

The soil, with proper culture, will produce every variety of vegetables, and is most grateful for kind treatment. Even with inferior cultivation, the soil yields a return that could not be realized in the most favored locality in the North, under the same treatment. For growing the orange, or any other semi-tropical fruit grown in Florida (north of the frost line), the Southern coast of Georgia, for sixty miles, has advantages over the orange district 100 miles south. The orange *tree* is more hardy, less liable to injury from cold, and the fruit has a thinner skin and higher flavor. I have 1,500 trees. Not a single year old seedling killed by the cold last January, while the trees in central and middle Florida suffered serious injury. Farm crops successfully grown are cotton, corn, sugar cane, sorghum, peas and beans, Irish and sweet potatoes, oats, rye, etc.

This region is far more healthy than any section of the North or West with which I am acquainted, and we have at St. Mary's as peaceable and law-abiding class of people—white and black—as can be found in any section. So far as I have seen, there is less sectional feeling in the South than in the North, and I have never had any fear of personal violence to myself, family or to any Northern man who may desire to settle in Georgia. For nearly ten years that I have lived South, I have, without exception, received the kindest treatment and evidences of good will.

The men who now represent the condition of society at the South to be such as should deter a Northern man from settling here, are enemies to the poor—white and black—North and South. Such men, who still appeal to the passions, were not clothed in blue or gray (during the civil strife) for honest purposes ; if wearing either color they were the *home guards*—or men seeking some personal benefit or political position. I have no doubt the persistent misrepresentations of the Southern people, has deterred many good men from seeking homes in the South ; who, could they have known the truth, would now be in the possession and enjoyment of free and independent homes in the South, freed from the anxieties of their present condition North.

Taxes in Pennsylvania and New York—where I have real estate interests—are as four to one in Georgia. In Georgia, taxes are low on a very low valuation—in the North they are high on a high valuation.

If all Georgians would work for Georgia as the Floridians work for Florida, the population would be doubled in ten years.

In my opinion there is no State in the Union that has the undeveloped wealth of Georgia. Every variety of fruit and grain grown in the United States can be successfully grown in Georgia ; its mineral wealth is very great, and its advantages for manufacturing everything useful are unsurpassed. Every variety of climate, from the balmy air on its Southern coast, to its mountains and snow of winter in the northern portion.

I am proud of my native State, New York, but equally as much interested in the prosperity and full development of my adopted State south.   *   *   *   *

SILAS FORDHAM,
St. Mary's, Camden county, Ga.

[Very interesting letters were also received from Mr. Joseph Sheppard, St. Mary's, a native of Pennsylvania; Mr. Richard Bealy, St. Mary's, from England; and Mr. W. A. White, St. Mary's, from Connecticut. The above covers the points fully, and is concurred in by the others.]

GLYNN COUNTY.

I am a lineal descendant of the seventh generation of Elder Wm Brewster, a native of Connecticut, and have resided here about ten years, and during the prevalence of yellow fever, was not sick at all. It prevailed here only by reason of a combination of circumstances of an extraordinary character, and which will probably never occur again. As it was, most persons could have avoided it as I did. I was educated a physician. Persons of various professions have visited and done business in our county and those adjoining, and are now settled and doing business here, apparently for life.

According to my knowledge and information, the inducements for immigration are fully equal to those of any quarter of the globe, and surpass those of most localities. The social condition is better than it is at the North. Better feeling prevails towards the North than is reciprocated. The South is more humble, which insures God's blessing. F. A. BREWSTER, M. D., Brunswick, Ga.

Massachusetts is my native State. I came here in 1865, and engaged in the manufacture of yellow pine lumber. My "profession" is pretty well filled up now. This section offers inducements to farmers, and especially to stock-growing. The climate is superior to that of Massachusetts, take it the year round. The soil, with care, is very productive of corn, cotton, vegetables and fruits of all kinds—bananas, olives, etc, wheat and all cereals. Health is good where the country is properly drained so that no stagnant ponds are near. This low, flat section must have drainage to insure health. The condition of society is every way satisfactory, and life is secure as anywhere. Taxes (local city) are moderately heavy—owing to extravagance of officials and unsatisfactory political condition after reconstruction, while under the temporary control of the negroes. The people are very kind to immigrants, and their social treatment is unexceptionable. Land is very cheap, and good farms are readily obtainable. WARREN A. FULLER, Brunswick, Ga.

[Reference is also made to Jno. R. Cook, Brunswick, Ga., from whom a letter was received.]

LIBERTY COUNTY.

It gives me pleasure to answer your questions. I was born in Rhode Island, and came here last December with my uncle, Mr. Coe. Am a farmer, and consider this the best place for a young farmer with small capital, on account of the cheapness of land, small cost of living and good prices for farm produce. The climate is healthy; have never been so well as since I came here. The soil *looks* good—time will tell *how* good. Rice, corn and cotton are the principal crops. Mine is all rice. Society is refined and agreeable, but very few white people in this section. It is perfectly safe for any *honest* man, white or black, to live here. I was cordially received, and all express a desire for settlers to come and "occupy the land." Lands worth from $1.00 to $5.00 per acre. G. A. BAILEY, Dorchester, Ga.

Not having been in Georgia a sufficient time to answer all your questions, I will confine myself to those which do not require length of time for solution. I am a farmer, came from New England in 1878. The inducements most noticeable to a new-comer are cheap lands for farming and grazing. From my brief experience, I consider the climate very healthy and enjoyable, and my life as safe here as in any place in our country. Think the freedmen are not so well able to withstand the temptation to steal as those who have had better opportunities for moral education.

The feeling manifested towards me has been most kind and cordial—Far more so than I had any right to expect. Found a hearty welcome everywhere.

I cannot refrain from saying that, in my estimation, there is no part of our country that possesses superior conditions for successful enterprise in any branch of farming, whether it be stock raising, farming proper or fruit growing. JAS. COE, Dorchester, Ga.

PIERCE COUNTY.

I came to Georgia in 1876, from Illinois. Am a physician, but find this section too healthy to be profitable for a man of my profession. The climate is very fine; soil rather lean. The productions are cotton, corn, sugar-cane, peas, potatoes, timber, turpentine. It is remarkably healthy. Society is rather poor, but life and property are perfectly safe. Taxes low. Good feeling towards immigrants, and they are well treated. The resources of this county are so undeveloped that it is difficult to say what may be accomplished; but that it is a natural fruit-growing country, especially for grapes, there is no doubt. Fruits and vegetables can be raised very profitably.

If properly cared for, sheep can be raised very profitably. The people are clever and peaceable, though generally illiterate; and there are but few schools.

Northern people can come here with entire safety. The laws are quite as well enforced as in the Northwest. I like this much better than Illinois and Michigan. For all diseases of the *air passages*, I do not think a better climate can be found.

W. E. FRASER, M.D., Blackshear, Ga.

[Letter also received from Mr. Daniel Campbell, Blackshear, Ga., fully sustaining the statements in the foregoing.]

WAYNE COUNTY.

Am a native of New York; came here in 1869, and engaged in merchandising. If goods are sold strictly for cash, I know of no better opening for well-posted business men than in Southeast Georgia. Little farming done in this immediate neighborhood, though climate and soil favor the production of cotton, rice, corn, oats, sugar cane and sweet potatoes. Soil in this county sandy, with clay subsoil. Crops are two or three weeks ahead of those across the river, in Liberty county (which is much lower than Wayne, but the richest and finest county in Southeast Georgia). Fruits grow in profusion and of elegant quality. This is as healthy a section as I ever lived in, and that covers a close acquaintance and sojourn in every State this side of Oregon and California. There are malarial fevers at times, but they readily succumb to ordinary remedies, and there is nothing of malignant type. Of the condition of society, can say nothing in its favor, but the adjoining county of Liberty has a splendid class of people, noted for morality.

Life and property are as safe as in any part of the United States. Taxes are unusually small, and we are out of debt, with a balance in the treasury. With a few exceptions among the most ignorant, the great majority of the people, and *all* the better classes extend a hearty welcome to Northern immigrants who are men of energy and industry. Capital, however, is no disqualification. With one-fourth the investment and one-fourth the labor here, a good farmer can reap *ten* times the value of the same investment North. Land can be bought at from 25 cents to $3.00 per acre.

During a residence of ten years, I have failed to see or hear of an instance, in this section, of "intimidation" or "shot-gun policy," to white or black. Perfect freedom of speech—political or religious. We need a *fence law* (to fence stock) and a dog law—for this country is magnificent for sheep-raising.

JAMES O. CLARKE, Doctor Town, Ga.

Want of space forbids the insertion of a very interesting letter from Mr. S. S. Moore, who came from Ohio in 1866. His post-office is Jesup, Ga.

INDEX.

A.

Appling County... 59
Agricultural College.. 19
Agricultural College, North Georgia.............................. 19
Aliens...22, 23
Atlanta, Temperature of.. 7
Atlanta University... 19

B.

Baker County... 49
Baldwin County..39, 41
Banks County...31, 33
Bartow County..32, 34
Berrien County... 49
Bibb County...39, 41
Brooks County..12, 49
Bryan County...59, 61
Bulloch County... 56
Burke County.. 56
Butts County..39, 42

C.

Calhoun County...49, 51
Camden County..59, 61, 62
Campbell County..39, 42
Carroll County...39, 43
Catoosa County.. 32
Charlton County...59, 61
Chatham County... 59
Chattahoochee County... 49
Chattooga County.. 32
Cherokee County... 32
Clarke County..39, 43
Clay County..12, 49, 51
Clayton County..39, 43
Clinch County... 59
Cobb County..32, 34

Coffee County.. 59
Columbia County..39, 43
Colquitt County.. 49
Coweta County..39, 44
Crawford County.. 49
Capacity of Soil under high Culture........................... 11
Climate.. 7
College of Agriculture... 19
Common Schools..20, 21
Constitution.. 21
Consumption... 17
Cotton... 10
Cotton Crop of Georgia.. 10

D.

Dade County...32, 35
Dawson County... 31
Decatur County... 49
DeKalb County.. 39
Dodge County... 56
Dooly County.. 49
Dougherty County...49, 52
Douglas County...39, 44

E.

Early County... 49
Echols County... 59
Effingham County..59, 61
Elbert County.. 39
Emanuel County.. 56
East Georgia... 56
Education.. 18
Emory College.. 19

F.

Floyd County...32, 35
Forsyth County..31, 36
Fannin County.. 31
Fayette County..39, 45
Franklin County.. 31
Fulton County...39, 45
Face of the Country.. 6
Female Colleges... 20
Fruits.. 11

G.

Gilmer County.. 31
Glascock County... 56

Glynn County...59, 63
Greene County...39, 46
Gordon County... 32
Gwinnett County... 31
Geographical Situation.. 5
Geologist, State... 15
Gold... 15
Gold Belt.. 16
Government.. 21

H.

Habersham County... 31
Hall County.. 31
Hancock County..39, 46
Haralson County..32, 36
Harris County.. 39
Hart County... 31
Heard County... 39
Henry County... 39
Houston County... 49
Health... 17
High Culture... 11

I.

Irwin County... 49
Indian Corn... 8

J.

Jackson County.. 31
Jasper County...39, 47
Jefferson County... 56
Johnson County... 56
Jones County... 39

L.

Laurens County... 56
Lee County... 49
Liberty County...59, 63
Lincoln County... 39
Loundes County...49, 52
Lumpkin County..31, 37
Lower Georgia..6, 9

M.

Macon County... 49
Madison County... 31
Marion County... 49
McDuffie County... 39

McIntosh County.. 59
Meriwether County.. 39
Miller County.. 49
Milton County... 31
Mitchell County.. 49
Monroe County.. 39
Montgomery County.. 56
Morgan County...39, 47
Murray County.. 32
Muscogee County...49, 52
Manual of Georgia..3, 4
Mercer University... 19
Metals and Minerals of Georgia...14, 33
Middle Georgia..6, 9, 39
Minerals and Metals of Georgia...14, 33
Mines.. 15

N.

Newton County... 39
Naturalization.. 22
Newspapers, List of...24, 25, 26, 27
North Georgia... 30
Northeast Georgia... 31
Northwest Georgia.. 32

O.

Oconee County...39, 47
Ogethorpe County..39, 48

P.

Paulding County..32, 37
Pickens County... 31
Pierce County..59, 64
Pike County.. 48
Polk County..32, 37, 39
Pulaski County..56, 57
Putnam County...39, 48
Pio Nono College.. 19
Population.. 16
Preface... 3
Public School System 20

Q.

Quitman County... 49
Qualification of Voters... 21

R.

Rabun County.. 31

Randolph County...49, 53
Richmond County...56, 57
Rockdale County... 39
Railroads in Georgia...27, 28
Religion 21

S.

Schley County...49, 53
Screven County...56, 58
Spalding County.. 39
Stewart County... 49
Sumter County... 49
Seamen... 23
Sectional Divisions.. 29
Soils and Productions... 7
Soils of Georgia.. 8
Southern Georgia.. 9
Southern Pacific Railroad.. 5
Southeast Georgia... 59
Southwest Georgia.. 49
Sugar Cane... 10
Summer Climate.. 7

T.

Talbot County.. 39
Taliaferro County.. 39
Tatnall County... 56
Taylor County...49, 54
Telfair County... 56
Terrell County..49, 54
Thomas County...49, 54
Towns County.. 31
Troup County...39, 49
Twiggs County... 56
Tobacco... 10

U.

Union County... 31
Upson County... 39
Upper Georgia...6, 8
University of Georgia.. 18
University, Mercer... 19
University, Atlanta.. 19

V.

Vegetables.. 11
Voters, qualification of... 21

W.

Walker County..32, 38, 49

Walton County..39, 49

Ware County.. 59

Warren County.. 39

Washington County..56, 58

Wayne County..59, 61, 64

Webster County.. 49

White County.. 31

Wilcox County.. 49

Wilkes County.. 39

Wilkinson County..56, 59

Whitfield County..32, 39

Worth County..49, 55

Winter climate.. 7